Red Canyon Red

Her friends jokingly call her 'Red Kenyon the Red Canyon Hellcat'. But the nickname isn't all in jest. The diminutive young woman with the unmanageable tangle of red hair has proved herself the equal of most men on more than one occasion.

But Red was only beginning to realize her mistake in trying to go after the stolen heifers alone. Far from any possibility of rescue or help, Leif Mortenson leers at the disarmed and helpless nemesis who has twice thwarted him. 'You've made a fool of me as many times as you get', he sneered. 'Now I get to have my fun, and there ain't nobody in the world that can keep me from it'.

As panic and despair wash over her, Red knows she has the toughest fight of her life ahead of her.

Red Canyon Red

Billy Hall

A Black Horse Western

ROBERT HALE · LONDON

© Billy Hall 2016
First published in Great Britain 2016

ISBN 978-0-7198-1808-0

Robert Hale Limited
Clerkenwell House
Clerkenwell Green
London EC1R 0HT

www.halebooks.com

The right of Billy Hall to be identified as
author of this work has been asserted by him
in accordance with the Copyright, Designs and
Patents Act 1988

Printed and bound in Great Britain by
CPI Antony Rowe, Chippenham and Eastbourne

CHAPTER 1

They all rolled out early for the shooting. Excitement was as palpable as the cool fog of morning. In spite of the hour, there was little of the normal yawning, scratching and stretching that usually accompanies early morning.

Only the wisp of a girl with too much hair seemed out of place. Her coarse pants, loose shirt and high-heeled boots were not in the least out of the ordinary. Only that thick, unmanageable thatch of red hair jutting from beneath the Stetson even made her look like a girl at all. Given the fact that not too many kept their hair cut very well anyway, she might well have passed for a young boy. The fact that she was a girl was well known to them all. She was, after all, the boss's daughter.

The rest of the group was as natural to the surroundings as the soap weed and sage brush. They wore a variety of hats, but all broad-brimmed against the Dakota sun. All sported the normal everyday duds of working cowboys.

All except one, that is. One among them obviously

paid more attention to personal hygiene and appearance. His preternaturally pale blue eyes were flat, devoid of expression. He was clean shaven, if, in fact, he was old enough to have the need to shave often. His clothes were better fitted than most. His black hat alone had no sweat stains discoloring the bottom half of the crown.

He wore his gun just a little differently, too. It would have been hard to quantify the difference. Maybe it was just too carefully positioned on his leg. Maybe its holster was just a bit too well-oiled and rubbed. Maybe the grips were polished by more consistent use than most. Whatever it was, there was that shade of difference. They all recognized it. None could have explained it, but they all knew what it meant. He was either a cowboy who was better than most with his gun, or he was a gunman passing himself off as a cowboy. The latter appeared the most likely.

Someone had already set up four rows of cans and bottles, six to a row. Two of the rows, side by side, were a little less than fifty feet from where they gathered. The other two rows, also side by side, were a good hundred yards away.

The slip of a girl with the big hair wore a holster that held a .41 caliber Colt. She wore it high on her waist, held by the same belt that supported the nondescript trousers. Too young to have the hips to support them, it was only the belt that kept the pants in place. She couldn't have been more than twelve.

It was her father who spoke. 'This here ain't no fast-draw contest,' he announced. 'It's just six shots apiece with the pistol, one at a time. Then six shots apiece with the rifle, one at a time. The one that busts the most bottles or holes the most cans wins.'

'What if they both get 'em all?' a voice queried.

'Then we'll set up some more an' do it again.'

'You givin' us a time limit?' the one who obviously considered himself a gunman demanded. 'I don't aim to stand here all mornin' while she aims that toy.'

The girl's father responded, with only the barest trace of a smile momentarily flitting across his face. 'That seems fair. We'll make it ten seconds from first shot to last.'

'I only need about three,' the gunman boasted.

'Then you hadn't oughta have any trouble at all with ten.'

'Who's goin' first?' one of the ranch hands asked.

'Let her go first,' the challenger said. 'I ain't in no hurry.'

The girl lifted her pistol from its holster. Even though it was smaller than the one favored by most men, it looked too big for her hand. She held it pointed at the ground. She looked at her father, brows raised.

Her father nodded. The girl lifted the gun and fired the six rounds it held in rapid succession. All six bottles shattered.

As if absent mindedly following some well-practised routine, she shucked out the empty brass and replaced them with fresh cartridges, then holstered the gun.

Eager to demonstrate his superiority, the challenger whipped his .45 Colt from its holster in a blur of speed.

Six shots, so closely spaced they sounded almost like one continuous roar, took barely over a single second. All six of his bottles broke. Only the last failed to shatter completely. The neck blew off it, leaving the rest of it standing. Still, it counted as a hit.

The girl's father handed her a small rifle. The .22 caliber Winchester looked more appropriate to her size than the pistol had. Without fanfare she lifted it to her shoulder and fired six evenly spaced shots, pumping the lever action of the rifle without moving it from her shoulder between shots. Three bottles shattered. Three cans leaped into the air and rolled a ways before stopping.

Almost instantly the .30-30 in the man's hand cradled against his shoulder and began firing. The roar of the large caliber rifle seemed inordinately loud after the crisp reports of the .22. Three bottles shattered. Two cans flew into the air. The other toppled over backward as the bullet plowed into the ground just in front of it. The bottom edge of the can was dented, but there was no hole in it.

A shout went up from every one of the observers. They crowded around the girl, clapping her on the back and congratulating her.

'Good shootin', Red!'

'I knowed you'd beat 'im, Red.'

'That oughta shut that braggadocio up.'

'You put 'im in 'is place, you did, kid.'

Unusual to the situation, no money changed hands. None of the cowboys had been willing to bet against the girl, so there were no takers to the freely advanced offers.

The vanquished gunman muttered something about a 'kid's gun' and stomped away toward the bunkhouse. The rest of the crew was at breakfast when he quietly rode out of the yard and headed down the road. Nobody grieved his absence, nor particularly cared where he went.

CHAPTER 2

The air was festive, but purposeful. More than three dozen cowboys milled about. Off to one side nearly 500 head of cows and calves crowded against one another. Cows bawled and bellowed for their calves. Calves, most roughly three months old, blatted and bleated in turn for their mothers.

Separating them was a job that required an inordinate amount of skill and finesse. Those with the best cutting horses deftly separated matched pairs of cow and calf, one pair at a time, from the rest of the herd. They worked slowly, methodically. Whenever it was evident which cow a calf belonged to, one of the riders would dab a rope on the calf and drag it to a branding fire.

Just over a quarter mile away, several cowboys formed a line that kept those already branded from managing their way back to the herd.

In between, another line of cowboys worked just as industriously to keep the calves in the herd from breaking free and dashing to the separated cows. Once a calf was branded and castrated, it was 'mothered up' again with the cow it belonged to. The pair would then dash off a short distance, then stop. The calf would begin to nurse and the cow would nibble at the well-trampled grass before wandering off.

Brands on horses being ridden indicated hands from the 777 Ranch, the Circle S, the 7-11 Ranch, the Rocking R, and the Heart R, as well as the host ranch, the X K Bar.

A dozen branding fires bristled with branding irons, heated and ready. Beside each fire three men on foot waited. As each calf was dragged to a fire, bawling and pulling against the lariat inexorably dragging it along, the cowboy would call out the brand and location he had read on the calf's mother.

'7-11. Left side.'

'Heart R. Left hip.'

'Rockin' R. Right hip.'

As soon as he did so, one of the hands on foot would grab the calf, lift it by a flank and throw it down on its side, with the side to be branded facing upward. He would instantly place a knee on the calf's neck, effectively pinning it to the ground.

The second man would grab a hind leg and plop down on the ground, sitting flat, facing the calf. One booted heel would be placed behind the knee of the lower leg. Pushing that leg forward with his foot, he would pull back on the top leg, stretching the calf helplessly on the ground.

Almost instantly another man with a hot iron would step over and apply the brand indicated. The calf would bawl and beller helplessly as the smell of burning hair and hide rose into the air.

Right behind the branding, the iron was placed back in the fire and that man would lift a knife from a bowl of water treated with Lysol, if the calf was male. He would swiftly sever the testicles, tossing them into a bucket placed there for that purpose.

Several times during the day one of the women would replace the bucket with an empty one, taking the filled ones to the cook shack. There they were cleaned by others of the women and readied to be fried at supper time. Every hand on every ranch looked forward hungrily to gorging on a meal of 'Rocky Mountain Oysters' at the end of every branding day.

It was hard, grueling, demanding, even dangerous work. Cows were prone to defend their calves fiercely. Horses fell or were tripped by an errant rope. On occasion a horse would spook at something and begin to buck, creating havoc in the immediate area. Accidental burns from branding irons were more common than anyone wished.

Even so, it was a time when area ranchers and their hands came together in common cause, creating an atmosphere of camaraderie unmatched anywhere. Jokes, jibes, compliments and ribald humor were tossed about freely. Rarely a fight would break out, but almost without exception it was between combatants where 'bad blood' already existed.

At one branding fire, during a brief wait for another calf, Lee Corson addressed Doug Kenyon. 'By Jing, Doug, that little slip of a girl o' yours does more work than any two hands in the bunch.'

Doug straightened, a hand on the small of his back, watching. As he did, Louellen gently moved her horse against a cow, forcing it slightly away from the calf that had begun to nurse at its side. As she pried her way between the two, the calf broke away and tried to dart in a circle around her to get back to its mother. Just as soon as it did, she whirled the loop of her lariat around her head once and sent the noose unerringly to settle over the calf's head. Her release of the loop was done with such a quick flick of her wrist that it almost looked as if that loop leaped forward of its own volition.

As the loop was settling over the calf's head, she had already jerked hard on it, so the loop closed over the animal's neck instantly. Even before it had done so she dallied the rope around her saddle horn and turned her horse toward the nearest branding fire, the calf jerking, bawling and complaining behind her. The lariat, stretched across the right leg of the chaps she wore, revealed the source of the well-rubbed mark about four inches wide across the thigh. Anyone seeing those rub marks on a pair of chaps never had to ask why cowboys wore them.

'Better slow down, Red,' the flanker at the branding fire teased. 'You're makin' some o' them cowboys look slow an' clumsy.'

Her quick grin flashed white in the middle of the

wildly flying red hair. 'What do you expect? They're just men,' she shot back. 'They don't have a chance. Do you need me to flank this one for you? He's kinda big.'

'Oh, I think I can manage this one all right.'

'She can flank a calf that weighs as much as she does,' a man who owned one of the represented ranches offered. 'I've seen her do it. When she was still little enough she couldn't hold it down, she flanked a bull calf over at Donaldson's brandin'. She flanked him down and hopped on his neck, and he just stood up anyway. She was sittin' a-straddle of his neck, holdin' on to both ears for all she was worth, when one of the guys flanked him down again.'

'Did she call him anything nice?'

'She was jawin' on 'im all right enough, but I don't rightly remember if she used any salty language.'

'I probably called him a cowboy that talked too much instead of getting calves branded,' Louellen suggested. 'Besides, I was only twelve years old then.'

'You ain't much bigger now!'

'So what? Do you think you can catch more calves in a day than I can?'

The rancher guffawed. 'I ain't gonna take that challenge, Red. When I was twenty years younger I couldn't match what you do in a day on top of a horse. I sure ain't gonna try now.'

As soon as her lariat was freed, she recoiled it and spun her horse around to head after another calf.

'I wonder how many horses she wears out in a day,' one of the cowboys pondered.

'Three, most days,' the rancher answered. 'Then they've all gotta have a day or two to rest afore she can use 'em again.'

'Her pa must have to run a whole remuda just to keep her in the saddle.'

The rest of the conversation was lost in the haze of dust and the bedlam of bawling cattle and yelling cowboys.

That Louellen – that little slip of a girl – proved herself as well as any cowboy could not be challenged.

CHAPTER 3

'I am not a child any longer, Father!'

'I'm very much aware of that, Louellen.'

'Then why can't I dress like a woman?'

'Do you realize how clumsy you'd be ropin' an' rasslin' calves wearin' a dress?'

'I don't need to wear a dress to look like a woman. They do make women's riding breeches, you know.'

Doug Kenyon snorted. 'Yeah, they do all right. The dumb things look like there's a gunny sack sewed on both sides, just below the waist.'

'They'd at least let me look like a woman.'

'They'd make you look like one o' them East high-fa-lutin' women that don't know nothin' but how to giggle an' impress some soft-handed dude. Why's it so danged important to look like a woman when you're workin' on a ranch anyway? When you get all dolled up for a dance or to go to town or church or whatever, you're the most fetchin' woman in the country. You don't need to flaunt it out here on the place.'

16

'Why not?'

'Coz I got a ranch to run, that's why not. It's hard enough keepin' a bunch o' hot-blooded, rambunctious cowboys' minds on their work without havin' 'em constantly tryin' to impress a good-lookin' woman.'

'They do anyway, in case you hadn't noticed,' she retorted.

'Your father's very much aware of that,' Xania Kenyon interjected. 'In fact, that's exactly what has your father upset.'

Louellen switched her gaze to her mother. The streaks of gray that modified the startling red of her mother's hair made it more than obvious from where her own copious tresses were inherited. Even those gray hairs did nothing to diminish the elder Kenyon woman's beauty. Her slender form still carried all the shapeliness of its youth. Her deep blue eyes had lost none of their twinkle. Though her name was Xania, almost nobody knew it. She thought it much too pretentious. She always and only went by Jenny. Even Louellen didn't know until recently that Jenny wasn't really her mother's name.

'Making me wear a man's clothes all the time doesn't hide the fact that I'm a woman,' Louellen retorted, her eyes pleading for her mother's support. 'You don't dress like this!'

Doug just as pointedly appealed to his wife, who still steadfastly refused to use her given name. 'Jenny, tell 'er how long you did, when we started up here.'

'I'll tell her how much I hated it, too,' Xania retorted. 'I felt like you were ashamed of me. I was getting heavy

17

with child before you allowed me to dress like I should have been dressing all along. You'd even have made me dress that way when we went to town if I'd have stood for it.'

An unexpected knock on the door interrupted the conversation. Doug strode to the door and jerked it open. Calvin Overstrander, youngest wrangler on the X K Bar, started to speak.

Before he could say anything, Doug bellowed, 'What do you want?'

Cal flinched but held his ground. He held his hat in front of him with both hands. He shifted from foot to foot. 'Uh, I'd like a word with Re … uh, with Louellen, if I might.'

Doug's jaw sagged open. He stared uncomprehendingly for a brief moment. His face suffused a steadily increasing shade. Xania stepped swiftly in front of him, physically crowding her husband back a step. Her voice was warm and welcoming.

'Of course, Cal. Step in, won't you?'

Looking sidelong at Doug as one might at an angry dog, Cal ducked inside the door. Xania put an arm around Doug's waist as if it were a mere affectionate gesture, but the pressure of her arm nearly pushed her husband off balance. Making it look as if it were a mutual idea, she propelled him toward the kitchen. Even as she did, she said, 'Louellen, there's someone here to see you.'

She needn't have made the announcement. Louellen was very much aware of the young cowhand's presence and had clearly heard him ask for her. Darting a grateful glance at her mother she hurried to the front room.

'Why, hello, Cal!' she said.

Doug's eyes flitted back and forth from the two in the front room to his wife. He opened his mouth to speak, but Xania motioned him to a part of the kitchen out of sight of the front door. He knew very well from her expression that her gesture was not to be ignored. As soon as they were out of the young couple's line of sight, he pointed a finger at the front room.

In a whisper that carried all the emotion of a shout he said, 'Jenny...'

Xania held up a hand, palm toward her husband. With a whisper every bit as demanding as his she said, 'Now, Douglas Dean! Our daughter is a young woman. It's only natural that she would have a caller. You had just as well get used to the idea.'

Sputtering as if a cactus were stuck in his throat, Doug said, 'Jenny! He's ... he's one of our hands!'

'I know that, dear. Would you prefer that some total stranger come calling on her?'

'But ... but ... but she's just...'

'She's just about the age I was when you came calling on me, as I remember,' she reminded him.

His eyes widened slightly. 'Yeah, and if he's thinking what I was thinking, I'll kill him!' he expostulated.

Xania giggled unexpectedly. She swiped a hand across her husband's head, mussing his hair and sending it forward across his face. He ran a hand through it, pushing it back somewhat into place. He swallowed hard. He took a deep breath.

'She can't be that old, yet,' he groaned.

Any answer was precluded by Louellen stepping into the kitchen. She cleared her throat to get their attention. She got it instantly. The intensity of that attention took her aback for a brief moment.

'Uh, Cal would like to escort me to the dance at the schoolhouse on Saturday. Will that be OK?'

It was fortunate that Xania had an answer ready. Doug would have been incapable of formulating an intelligible one.

'Are you comfortable going with him?' she asked.

'Oh, yes,' Louellen answered instantly. 'He's always a perfect gentleman.'

'Then I don't know why not,' Xania replied. 'Will you be riding or taking the buckboard? Your father doesn't know it yet, but he's using the buggy to take me to the dance.'

'I … I don't know if he's even thought about that,' Louellen admitted.

'It might be best if you both just rode your horses,' Xania offered. 'That way your father won't be worrying about the two of you in the back of the buckboard on the way home.'

'Mother!' Louellen shouted in an offended whisper, her face suddenly bright red.

Laughing at her daughter's discomfiture, Xania said, 'Just tell him yes if you want to go with him,' she said, motioning her daughter back toward the front room.

Doug simply stood through the whole conversation,

looking much like a fish out of water, his mouth opening and closing silently a dozen times. The two of them talked long into the night about the realities of their little cowgirl growing into a young woman.

CHAPTER 4

'Sure a lot o' rough-lookin' guys I ain't never seen afore,' Doug remarked.

'It does seem like an awfully rough crowd,' his wife agreed. 'Are you sure the kids will be all right?'

'The kids? You mean them two you been tellin' me were all growed up adults?'

'Well, they are! But they aren't, really. I mean …'

He chuckled. 'Now, Jenny, don't go sputterin'. I might think I got the best of ya.'

Xania elbowed her husband in the ribs. 'I'm serious, Doug. Do you think they'll be all right? I don't know where all these people have come from.'

'Dances ain't like they was afore they went an' found tin in the area,' he agreed. 'Now it's the same get-rich-quick bunch that flocked in when it was gold they was after. Do you know there's thirteen saloons in Hill City again? We was down to three after the gold craze petered out. Now we're back up to thirteen!'

'You still didn't answer my question.'

'Yeah, they'll be fine. We'll sorta keep an eye on 'em.'

'At least they asked if they could just ride along with us, and follow our buggy. That surprised me.'

'Me too. I'm guessin' maybe Cal knowed there'd be a lot o' the minin' crowd an' likely a bunch o' the riffraff here.'

'It'll be especially good to have them that close on the way home when it's late and all those people have been passing around too many bottles.'

The crowd was far larger even than they expected. The schoolhouse was so crowded less than half the folks could find space inside at one time. People drifted in and out steadily. The dance area was crowded enough couples constantly bumped into one another. A couple of minor fights had erupted as a result, but were quickly quelled by others. 'Minor miner mix-ups,' some wag had termed them.

Three fiddles and an accordion made up what passed for the dance band. Two of the fiddlers and the accordion were surprisingly accomplished. The third fiddler struggled to keep up and follow, but the others encouraged him. From time to time an older man with a harmonica joined in.

Somebody called out, 'All right, folks. Get divided up into groups of eight and we'll do a little square dancin'.'

'Is Andy gonna call it?' someone yelled out.

Sudden silence fell over the crowd as all eyes turned to a man of around fifty seated on a bench along the wall. He stood up slowly. 'Yeah, I'll call it, if you'll all do what I call,' he challenged, his eyes twinkling mischievously.

Several whoops and hollers attested to his popularity among those who liked square dancing. In short order the groups were formed and the music started. It was quickly apparent why Andy had issued the challenge. He started routinely enough to allow everyone to get into the swing of things, then started tossing in unexpected allemande lefts and do-si-dos, promenades and star by the right and balance left until he had nearly made contortionists of the dancers, who laughed so hard they could barely hear his instructions. The mood was festive, almost to the point of hilarity.

It was loud enough none of those inside, and only a few of those outside even heard the shots.

Christopher Coleman, a hand on the 777 Ranch, had brought a girl from town. Heidi Sorensen was the daughter of the saddle maker in Hill City. She was Louellen's best friend, but she and Christopher were not inclined to square dance. Cal and Louellen joined one of the square dance groups, while their friends took the opportunity to get away from the crush of people and go for a walk.

The quiet of the night contrasted sharply with the loud gaggle of noises from the schoolhouse. They talked quietly as they walked, hand in hand, unaware they had gone quite a distance from the crowd.

'Well, lookee what we got here!'

The harsh voice, only slightly slurred, brought them up short. Clearly visible in the moonlight, four coarsely dressed men faced them in a semi-circle. One held an open bottle. All wore guns.

Softly Chris told Heidi, 'Just turn around and walk back toward the crowd.'

They had gone less than a dozen steps when the quartet appeared as if by magic, squarely in front of them, again blocking their path. 'Now that ain't in the least bit sociable,' the one who had spoken previously admonished them. 'What's the hurry?'

'Please let us past,' Heidi blurted.

Three of the four laughed. The fourth said, 'Well, we might consider doin' that if we was to get paid a small toll for the use o' this here path. How about one kiss apiece from the purty girl?'

The other three laughed again. Speechless, the young pair stared from face to face. Christopher said, 'That ain't even funny. Now stand aside.'

'And what're you gonna do if we don't?' the spokes-man demanded.

Before he could even answer one of the others said, 'I ain't settlin' for no kiss. She's a fine-lookin' one, she is. There's plenty there for all four of us.'

Heidi gasped at the audacity with which the threat was spoken, as if it were a matter of no great import.

Christopher spoke softly, urgency giving even the softly spoken words a sharp edge. 'Go to my left and run as fast as you can go. Head for the crowd and scream bloody murder. I'll hold 'em as long as I can.'

Before she could move one of the quartet said, 'Save yourself the trouble, little lady. We'll just shoot 'im. Then he won't get to watch us enjoy what he's been hopin' to get.'

'Go!' Christopher commanded, shoving her to his left.

Before she could move a quiet voice to Christopher's right said, 'There's no need to run. Chris, take Heidi and go on back to the dance.'

All eyes swung to the intruder. Shannon Creed stepped out of the trees and took a stance less than a step from Coleman. He stood there looking perfectly relaxed, but his hand hovered just against the butt of the .45 tied down on his leg.

'Go on, you two,' he said evenly to the couple. 'Now.'

Glancing back and forth once between Creed and the quartet, Christopher took hold of Heidi's elbow and propelled her to the side.

Just as he did the spokesman of the quartet said, 'Take 'im, boys!'

All four grabbed for their guns. Christopher pulled Heidi into a full run as the roar of gunfire erupted. He had no idea how many shots he heard. It sounded like war had broken out. Deathly silence followed as abruptly as the gunfire had exploded.

Heidi jerked her arm away and stopped, turning around. Christopher grabbed for her to force her to run again. As he did he looked back the way they had come, less than a dozen running steps before. Creed stood in the path. The moonlight made the wisp of smoke rising from his gun barrel seem ghostly.

Christopher blinked and shook his head. It took him several seconds to realize all four of their assailants were lying still on the ground.

Jaw agape, he stared at Creed. 'How did you...?'

In a voice that sounded more tired than anything, Creed said, 'Go on back to the dance. I think the sheriff is there. You might send him out here.'

Christopher and Heidi looked at each other, then back at Creed.

'Are you all right?' Heidi demanded.

'I'm fine. They weren't all that fast,' Creed said. 'Now run along. I'll wait for the sheriff.'

The pair started to walk back toward the school-house, but found themselves running for all they were worth without even realizing it. A few of those outside had heard the shots and were looking in their direction. At Heidi's screams, people's attention was arrested enough that even some of the dancers rushed outside to see what was going on. The music inside stopped.

'The sheriff!' Christopher kept calling out. 'We need the sheriff!'

They were still well away from the schoolhouse door when a man stepped in front of them. Garth Emerson said, 'Whoa, there. Why're you hollerin' for me, young man?'

The pair jerked to a stop. Breathing hard Christopher said, 'Sheriff, there's been a shooting. There was four men—'

Heidi interrupted. 'Sheriff, they were going to kill Chris and take me and ...'

The two began talking over the top of each other until nothing either one said could be discerned.

Garth held up a hand. 'Whoa, whoa! Slow down! Heidi Sorensen, what're you doin' out yonder in the timber anyway? Are your folks here? Who's this guy you're with? Do your folks know you're with him?'

'Yes, yes. They're here. Chris works on the 777. We told Father. Chris and I just went for a walk to get some fresh air and get away from the crowd. Then these four men stopped us and they told Chris they were going to take me and … and—'

'They said if I tried to stop them they'd just shoot me and take her anyway,' Chris jumped in. 'I told Heidi to run and I'd try to hold 'em off long enough for her to get away.'

'You ain't even wearin' a gun,' the sheriff noted.

'No, sir. I was just comin' to a dance. I wasn't lookin' for … I mean …'

'So what stopped 'em?'

'I ain't sure who he is,' Christopher said. 'I should know 'im, I think, but it was dark and it all happened so fast and …'

'Shannon Creed,' Heidi offered.

Garth grunted. 'How'd he get mixed up in this?'

'I don't know,' Christopher said. 'All at once he was just there beside me and I didn't know anyone else was around. He told us to come back to the dance. One of the guys that stopped us said something like "Get 'im, boys," then there were a lot o' shots real fast, then nothin'. We stopped and looked and the guy…' He looked at Heidi, then bobbed his head. 'Creed. Yeah. You're right. That's who it is. I knew I should know 'im.

Creed was just standin' there and the other guys were … well, dead, I guess. They weren't movin' anyway.'

'He said he'd wait there for you,' Heidi said. 'He told us to go get you and tell you what happened, and he'd wait there.'

Others who had gathered around to listen were already headed back the way the pair had appeared. With a sigh Garth said, 'All right. You kids go on back to the dance. Tell your folks what happened, young lady. Your pa's gonna blame me for not keepin' a lid on things, sure's shootin'. I'll take care o' things.'

'Creed has a ranch between here and 777,' Christopher said. It was more of a statement than a question.

Garth nodded. 'Mighty lucky for you he's the one that noticed you two wanderin' too far away from everyone. At least that's my guess as to why he showed up just then. I'll know more directly.'

'Is he really that good with a gun?' Christopher asked, his voice tinged with awe.

'Yeah, and then some,' Garth said as he walked away.

'Heidi! Heidi, is something wrong?' Louellen Kenyon called out as she approached on a run.

Heidi whirled at the sound of the voice. She lunged toward the safe haven of a trusted friend. The two clung to each other a long moment. The presence of her friend broke the shock of all that had happened, and Heidi collapsed in tears. She sobbed out the whole story as Louellen attempted to soothe her.

Cal joined a couple of others in questioning

Christopher, getting the story from him as well. By the time the pair had told their story several times, the information had made its way to those who had stayed inside. Soon the schoolhouse emptied entirely into the yard, excited voices replacing the prior sounds of music and gaiety.

Stories that ran the gamut from mundane to near mythological buzzed through the crowd. Those who knew Creed's background, or knew him personally, became instant celebrities. The rest clamored for more and more information. Within an hour, more had been told about the man than a dozen men could possibly have done in a lifetime.

Not long afterward Doug Kenyon decided it was time for his family to head home. The ride home was largely silent between Doug and Xania. The steady hum of voices from the pair following along on horseback indicated Cal and Louellen were finding much more to talk about.

To Cal's chagrin, however, it was more about Shannon Creed than anything he had done. 'Some way to impress the boss's daughter,' he lamented silently.

CHAPTER 5

Cowtowns are always hungry for a little entertainment. Word passed around quickly that the Kenyon family was coming to town for groceries and supplies today. That was no big deal. What mattered was that the Kenyon girl had let it be known she was planning to accept Hugh Matterson's challenge to a shooting match. It would take place in the area facing the big cliff behind Owen Hantsberger's gunshop.

Even more exciting, she had opened it up to a contest with anyone else that wanted to pit his (or her, although it was unlikely there would be another 'her' represented) speed and skill against her.

During the week preceding the event, bets began to be placed, and arguments about the relative skills of various people were waged fervently.

The day of the big match, an air akin to that of a circus coming to town pervaded. All thirteen saloons of Hill City nearly emptied. Eleven men had advanced their names to compete against 'that redheaded slip of a girl from the X K Bar.' There would probably be a few more that would step forward.

Sheriff Garth Emerson was agreed upon as the official timer. Each contestant would have six cans to shoot at, at one hundred yards' distance. To qualify, all six had to be holed. Any that were hit on an edge and dented but not holed would not count. Each would have one turn. Each would begin shooting when Garth said 'Go.' Garth would time each from the time he did so until the sixth can was hit. If a can was missed, the shooter was free to shoot at it more than once. It was generally accepted, however, that having to take even one extra shot would almost certainly ensure that shooter's loss of too much time for which to compensate.

It didn't take all that long. Because she was the one issuing the challenge, Louellen was the last one to shoot. After each contestant had hit all six cans, Tom Hagen walked the hundred yards and set up six more cans, or the same cans, since it didn't matter how many holes they ended up with. It was clearly obvious when a shot hit one. Tom was careful to put each can in the exact spot its predecessor had occupied, to be sure everything was fair. Almost all the time of the contest was spent waiting for Tom to walk the hundred yards, set up the cans, and walk the hundred yards back again.

After each shooter Garth announced that contender's time. Though it probably wasn't necessary, he also wrote each one down in a small notebook he kept in his shirt pocket.

One by one the shooters did their best. Then it was

Louellen's turn.

To be perfectly fair, she might have had a slight advantage. Her .22 caliber Winchester was smaller and lighter, and the recoil considerably less than those any of the others used. The others, with one exception, used either a .30-30 or a .44-40. The lone exception was Leif Mortenson, a known gunman. He used his Colt .45, with a detachable rifle stock attached.

Mortenson had only begun showing up locally the past few months, after a goodly while when nothing of him was seen or heard. He looked older, harder than when he left. In addition to the Colt .45 he had always worn, he now boasted a second similar weapon, worn on the left side of his belt, butt forward. Just behind it a large Bowie knife made him appear over-armed for any good purpose. Nobody seemed to know who he worked for, if anyone, or what he did for a living. The only people seen to associate with him were hard cases and riffraff.

The rifle Louellen used was a model new enough to be novel. It had a pump action instead of a lever action as the larger caliber rifles had. That made it easier and quicker to reload after each shot without her having to move it from her shoulder. That also allowed her to keep her aim steady enough; it required very little adjustment between shots.

Because of using his .45 with a detachable stock, Mortenson was relieved of the necessity of cocking the gun after each shot, so he was the fastest among the contestants. Even so, when Garth announced the times,

Louellen was a full second faster than Mortenson.

The gunman looked as if he wanted to challenge the accuracy of Garth's timekeeping, but ended up simply glaring at the lawman and walking away. Louellen well remembered him as the young hand her father had hired a few years earlier. He had ridden out the day she defeated him in a shooting match at the ranch. She hadn't seen him since. As his pale eyes fell momentarily on her a shiver ran up her back.

She didn't have time to dwell on it. Several people stopped to slap her on the back or congratulate her, but the crowd dissipated so swiftly it seemed almost magical that the space so lately crowded was silent and empty. It appeared as if everyone present had sudden business to attend to. Most of it was in the plethora of saloons where every shot would be rehashed a dozen times, bets paid off, and, before the day was over, more than one fight would erupt over some perception of the match.

Her father having gone to get the team and buckboard for the trip home, Louellen was left suddenly alone. Or so she thought. Nothing seemed to move except one lone tumbleweed that rolled along the ground. The voice just behind her startled her.

'If you wanta be a mite faster, keep both eyes open.'

Louellen whirled to look at the soft voice that spoke behind her. Her face colored with instant anger, though it didn't approach the color of her hair.

'I beat 'em all, didn't I?' she demanded.

The newcomer smiled. 'Yup. You did for a fact. Some of 'em weren't just too happy to get whipped by a girl.'

'You forgot the part about a "little slip",' she shot back.

He chuckled. 'Oh. Sorry. Your folks didn't tell me it was official to refer to you as a "little slip of a girl".'

'Everyone else seems to know it.'

He nodded his head slightly. 'It does come to mind that I've heard the term used when you were the subject of conversation.'

'And just who was so occupied with talking about me?'

'Oh, just about everyone, now an' then. Especially after you show up all these proud cowboys by outshootin' 'em. Or outridin' 'em. I heard about you ridin' Cyclone.'

The flush came back to Louellen's face, but it had lost its angry shade. Her voice took on an exaggerated drawl. 'I suppose it went something like, "Why, that little slip of a girl actually stayed on that horse as well as a big strong man might have".'

He laughed. 'I don't remember the strong man part.'

'My father won't admit it, but I think he won almost fifty dollars when I rode that horse.'

'Is that so? I only made twenty-four.'

Her mouth dropped open as her eyes widened. 'You bet on me?'

'Yup.'

'Why?'

'Seen you ride before.'

'When?'

He shrugged. 'Don't matter. Seen you shoot before, too. Like I said, you need to practice keepin' both eyes open.'

She frowned. 'But if I have both eyes open it'd be harder to just look down the sights.'

He shook his head. 'Just till you get used to doin' it right. With both eyes open you can see everything, not just the target, so you can find the target quicker. Once you've done it that way for a while, you'll see everything normal, but it'll look like the sights are just there, and you can see what's movin' on the edges of your vision as well. It's a lot quicker.'

Louellen's chin lifted. Her lips pressed into a thin line. 'And I suppose you're going to tell me you could outshoot me. I didn't see you among the ones challenging me today.'

He shrugged. 'I don't generally do stuff like that.' His eyes took on a distinct twinkle. 'Besides, I didn't want to show you up.'

'Oh, is that it? How very gallant of you! Well, if you're so good, why don't you show me how much better and faster it is to shoot your way? Everybody seems to be gone now, so you won't embarrass this poor little slip of a girl.'

He studied her face for a long minute. 'If you really want me to, I guess we could do that. There's half a dozen cans still layin' over there to the left. There's some more a ways to the right. They already got holes in 'em, but we'll know if we hit 'em when they fly up in the air.'

'And who's going to time us, to see who hits all six first?'

His smile was almost suppressed, but she could see

the corners of his mouth twitching.

'You think that's funny! Do you actually think you're so much faster than I am that we won't even need a timer?'

The smile pushed a little harder to express itself. 'I guess we'll just have to see,' he said.

She glared daggers at him for the better part of a minute, then whirled toward the targets a hundred yards distant. She jerked her rifle to her shoulder. In rapid fire she sent six cans flying into the air. With a triumphant look she turned wordlessly toward him.

He stepped half a step forward. His rifle flew to his shoulder. Six shots erupted from his rifle barrel so quickly the first can was still moving when the sixth one rose into the air. In silence he thumbed half a dozen cartridges from his gun-belt and refilled the rifle's magazine.

When he had reloaded his gun he lifted his eyes to hers. She was still standing, slack-jawed, staring at him.

'That's not even possible!' she breathed. 'You can't... Nobody can... How can you even aim that fast, let alone lever a new shell in every time?'

'Part of it's keepin' both eyes open,' he said.

'Red! Better come along!'

The voice of Louellen's father from the road turned her attention away. She waved. 'I'm coming, Father! I'll be right there.'

She waited for her father to wave his response, then turned back, but the man who had just displayed an impossible feat of gunmanship was no longer there. She looked around frantically, more startled by his absence than she had been by his presence there after everyone else was gone. Try as she might she could see no trace of him.

'He must have gone into the back door of Owen's gunsmith shop,' she muttered. 'That's the closest place. But why did he disappear so quick? I know Father knows him, but I have the impression Mother doesn't like him too well.'

By the time she had walked to where her parents waited with the buckboard, however, her mind had turned to other things. Several times on the way home she thought of him, but it was the idea of learning to sight with both eyes open that kept occupying her mind. His face remained as clear in her mind as the fluffy cloud that cast a brief shadow across the ground. It was destined to become much more familiar.

CHAPTER 6

'It was just called Seim's Mine for quite a while.'

Fork suspended halfway to her mouth, Louellen asked, 'I thought it was always called the Broken Boot.'

Creed frowned thoughtfully for a long moment. 'I guess I don't rightly know when they started callin' it that. Somebody tagged the name onto it, and the name just stuck. Nobody hardly knows what Seim's Mine is any more.'

'Sorta strange how that happens,' Doug Kenyon observed around a generous bite of backstrap smothered in gravy. 'Boy, this is one fine bit o' venison. There ain't nothin' in the world any better'n fried backstrap, mashed spuds an' gravy.'

Shannon had ridden into the place in the early afternoon, bearing a haunch of venison and one full backstrap. It had become almost a weekly occurrence for him to visit, always bringing something to prevent the visit from appearing to be mooching a meal. There was never any doubt who he was really coming to see.

'Deer are gettin' pretty scarce,' Shannon bemoaned. 'If the mines keep producin' well enough to keep this many people in the hills, there ain't gonna be any left at all.'

'So what happened at the Broken Boot?' Louellen brought the conversation back to her point of interest, impatience giving the faintest edge to her voice.

'Which boot is that?' Creed asked, leaning over to look at her boots beneath the table. His feigned wide-eyed innocence failed to hide the mischievous twinkle. 'Did you bust the heel off of one of yours or something?'

Louellen stamped her foot impatiently under the table. 'You know very well what I'm asking. Now stop teasing and tell me the story.'

'Well, if I tell the whole story, my supper'll get cold, so here's the short version. It seems the mine produced steady – but not too great – tons of iron pyrite …'

'That's fool's gold.'

'Yup.'

'So what good is that?'

'Well, the fact is it takes a lot o' sulfuric acid to process gold ore. Iron pyrite's the easiest source of the stuff needed to make the acid. So they was makin' a whole lot more money sellin' the pyrite than they was the gold. So they decided to just squirrel away the gold they were diggin' and run the mine on the income from the pyrite. They had more'n a year's worth piled up when they decided to go ahead and ship it. Trouble is, there was three guys workin' for 'em that'd figured out what they was doin', and watchin' for 'em to do somethin' with it. When they did, they set up a trap an' stole the whole kit an' caboodle.'

Louellen gasped. 'The whole year's worth of gold?'

'Yup.'

'So where did you come in?'

'Well, before the dust was hardly settled, they came to me and asked me to go after 'em. They said they'd be right generous if I'd get their gold back.'

The eyes of three Kenyons studied his face intently. 'They didn't say what generous meant?'

'Nope.'

'And you didn't ask?'

'Nope. They was honest folks. Didn't figure I needed to. Anyway those three weren't too hard to track at all. I caught up with 'em just as they was buryin' it, plannin' to wait till things blew over, then come back an' dig it up.'

'You arrested all three of them, single-handed?' Louellen gasped again.

He shook his head. 'They didn't take kindly to that idea. But they did have a nice big hole dug, so I just buried 'em in it an' took the gold back to Seims an' Nelson. They kept their word, like I knew they would. They were more than just generous. They gave me a third of it.'

Doug whistled. 'That is generous. Especially since they hadn't promised anything specific.'

'That was just what I needed, too. I'd been savin' up just as much as I could from what I could make as a shotgun guard, a little bounty huntin', an' that. With what they gave me for gettin' back their gold, I was able to get a pretty good start on my ranch.'

'Well, I'm plumb glad you chose where you did to start it. Can't think of anyone I'd rather have as a neighbor.'

'Thanks,' Creed said, trying to minimize the effect an undercurrent of emotion threatened to reveal in his voice. 'Some folks ain't been that kind about a guy with the reputation of a gunfighter for a neighbor.'

The conversation continued through supper and beyond, until Creed said, 'It's gettin' late. I've overstayed my welcome long enough. I'll be headin' home.'

In a complete reversal of her initial dislike of the man, Xania assured him, 'You'll have a hard time over-staying your welcome here. You're more than welcome anytime.'

Half an hour later Creed led his saddled horse out of the barn and prepared to mount. A slight motion in the darkness sent his hand streaking to his gun.

'Don't go shootin' me! It's just me, Cal,' Cal Overstrander announced. 'Didn't mean to startle you.'

'How you doin', Cal?'

'Well, fair to middlin', I guess.'

'Somethin' on your mind?'

'Well, yeah, as a matter o' fact, there is. Me'n Van an' Flint been noticing that you been shovin' your feet under the boss's table on a pretty regular basis lately. We're just gettin' concerned. You ain't got designs on the boss's daughter, by any chance, do you?'

The gathering darkness served to conceal the faint grin, as Creed carefully verified the position of all three men. In spite of what might have been a threatening situation, he felt himself to be in no peril.

'Well, I guess I'd be lyin' if I said I didn't,' he acknowledged. 'But for whatever it's worth, those designs are totally honorable. We ain't officially courtin' or nothin', so the field's wide open. You boys are just as free to win her heart if you can. Same rules apply, though. If any of you does anything dishonorable, or anything to hurt that girl, you'll answer to me.'

A long silence ensued, followed by the shuffling of feet sidling away.

'That's fair enough, I guess,' Cal said, his voice betraying the fact that he wasn't at all happy about it.

Creed stepped into the saddle. 'Well, you boys have a good evenin'. Unless I miss my guess you're likely to have venison steak for supper tomorrow, so don't be late when Frenchy rings the supper bell.'

'You got a deer?'

'Yeah, I popped a nice young buck just over the top o' Cooney's Ridge yesterday. Fine eatin'. Don't be late for supper.'

He touched his heels to his horse and trotted out of the yard, silently pondering whether he had anything substantive to fear from any of the X K Bar crew. He decided he had enough threats from enough directions, they'd just have to get in line. If they wanted to discourage him from courting the most beautiful young woman in the country, they'd have to do a lot more than just get in line.

CHAPTER 7

The greatest of times can turn to tragedy in a heartbeat.

The three-day cattle drive had taken four days. No matter. They were in no hurry. It would have been easier to just drive the steers to Deadwood to sell than herding them all the way to Cheyenne. Doug Kenyon wasn't sure why he wanted to sell them in Cheyenne instead.

The money they brought would be almost the same. Probably not quite, though. Booming as it was, the population of Deadwood wasn't large enough to accommodate that many cattle in one bunch. Cheyenne, on the other hand, had almost limitless capacity.

Mostly, Doug wanted to go to Cheyenne. Xania had no desire for the larger city. In fact, she almost panicked whenever it was necessary for her to do so. She had only been to Cheyenne three times since she and Doug married, and she would be perfectly content to let that be the total for the rest of her life.

Louellen, on the other hand, was eager to experience what the city had to offer. She especially wanted to see one of the operas or stage plays that were regularly offered there. Her father was more than willing to provide her that experience. Accordingly, he and Louellen remained in Cheyenne after the rest of their crew returned home.

As chance would have it, the 500-seat Cheyenne Theatre was featuring the final nightly show of Edmund Audran's hit farcical comic opera *Olivette*. The troupe had performed it for more than a year at London's Royal Strand Theatre at Westminster. They were scheduled to open the following week at Denver's Tabor Grand Opera House.

Her father had relented and allowed her to wear a dress and act like a woman for a change, instead of always pretending to be a boy. It was almost as thrilling to notice all the looks and attention she garnered as the opera itself.

The hit song was *The Torpedo and the Whale*, about a love-smitten whale who mistook a Woolwich torpedo for a rival.

Louellen laughed until her sides hurt, and she and her father talked about it far into the night after they returned to their hotel room. She found, to her surprise, that she could remember and sing almost the entirety of the song that was the centerpiece of the farce.

At her urging they decided to stay yet another night in Cheyenne, just so they could try out the food at a nearby restaurant a number of people had raved enthusiastically about.

'Are you sure the money's safe in our hotel room?'

Louellen Kenyon's voice conveyed the gravity of her concern, as they prepared to go to supper.

'Oh, I think so,' her father assured her.

The tone of his voice was clearly designed to allay her fears. She was not convinced.

'But if Cheyenne is such a dangerous place that I have to dress like a man, what makes you think our money's safe in the room?'

He shrugged. 'It's well hidden, and there shouldn't be anyone that even knows there's any there. We'll just be gone long enough to get some supper anyway. We ain't gonna be near as late gettin' back as we was last night.'

They were less than a block from the hotel when her worst fears were realized.

A loud voice, laden with a mixture of fear and anger, cried out, 'Leave me alone!'

The eyes of father and daughter whipped around at the fright and outrage in the woman's voice.

'Aw, c'mon, honey,' a rough voice responded. 'You too good fer me or what?'

A woman jerked in vain to wrest her arm from the large man's grip. She had every appearance of being a perfectly respectable young woman. The man obviously thought otherwise.

'I got me a room right over there at the hotel,' he told her, his eyes running up and down her body hungrily. 'I got money enough to take ya fer the whole night.'

'I am not that kind of woman!' she insisted. A note of panic crept into her voice. 'Unhand me!'

Oblivious to her objections, he began to propel her across the street. She fought back as best she could, but her strength was no match for his.

'Somebody! Help me! Please!' she yelled.

Doug Kenyon stepped into the street in front of the pair. 'Better leave her be,' he cautioned the roughly dressed cowboy.

The man stopped, glaring at Doug. 'This ain't none o' your affair,' he growled.

'Oh, I guess it prob'ly is if a lady asks for help,' Doug disagreed. His voice took on a sharper tone. 'Now let loose of her and head on down the street. There's several saloons down that way that'll have what you're lookin' for.'

'I found what I'm lookin' for.'

'No, I'm afraid you haven't. Turn her loose.'

'I told you this ain't none o' your business. Now butt out or you'll wish you had.'

Doug's hand brushed the butt of the Colt .45 at his hip. He shook his head. 'I guess I just made it my business. Let her go.'

'Big mistake, mister,' the man said. He shoved the woman away. His hand blurred upward, his pistol already in its grip. Doug grabbed for his own weapon much too late. It wasn't clear of leather when the stranger's gun belched fire and lead. The slug slammed into Doug's chest, driving him backward.

'Father!' Louellen screamed, rushing toward him.

By the time she reached him he was crumpled in the dirt of the street. The woman who had been freed from the man's grip stood stock still, both hands in front of her mouth, as if physically holding back the scream that threatened to emerge.

'I told 'im to butt out,' the man boasted.

Louellen grabbed the heavy Colt from her father's limp hand. Gripping it with both hands, she lifted it, thumbing the hammer back even as she did so. A look of disbelief crossed the stranger's face for an instant before the large pistol in Louellen's dainty hands jumped and barked. He took a step backward. He started to lift his gun toward the delicate looking youngster, who gripped the gun that looked far too large for those petite hands. A second bullet slammed into him, then a third so closely behind the second the echoes of all three shots bounced against each other as they caromed off the storefronts.

The gunman flopped backward onto the street. A small cloud of dust erupted around him, then settled back to earth.

Louellen dropped her father's gun and whirled back to his prone figure. She grabbed his head and lifted it. 'Father! Father!' she pleaded. 'Don't die, Father. I'll get you to a doctor.'

Her father's eyes focused with difficulty on her face. He struggled to speak. 'Get ... get the money back to your Ma, Red. She ... she needs ...'

Whatever else he was trying to say was drowned out by a bright red, frothy geyser spewing from his mouth. His eyes went flat. His body sagged into the dirt.

'What's goin' on here?' a harsh voice demanded.

Louellen looked up into the frown of a man whose badge shone prominently from the front of his vest. She tried to speak, but her voice caught in her throat. Tears coursed down her cheeks.

The woman who had been in the gunman's grasp spoke up. 'He tried to help me, Marshal,' she said. Her voice was surprisingly composed. She waved a gloved hand at the body of her pursuer. 'This man obviously thought I was a ... an available ... woman. He was forcing me toward the hotel with him. I cried out for help. This man intervened, and was summarily shot for his trouble. Then his ... his son ... I believe ... you called him Father?'

Louellen found her voice. 'He's my father,' she said, fiercely choking back the sob that threatened to leave her speechless.

The woman nodded. 'You're a girl!'

'I am a woman!' Louellen retorted. 'Father wanted me to dress this way to be safer while we were in Cheyenne.'

'You shot him!' the woman said, still just as stunned.

'Of course I shot him. He murdered my father!' she wailed.

The woman turned her attention back to the marshal. 'He ... I'm sorry. She ... grabbed her father's gun and shot this ruffian,' she explained. 'And fully and entirely justified it was!'

The marshal looked around at the circle of the curious that had inevitably formed. 'Anyone else see it?'

'Just exactly like she said,' some man who looked like

a merchant announced. 'I didn't even have time to get involved afore it was all over and done, but it's just like she said.'

Several voices offered their assent and agreement. The marshal nodded. 'Where are you from, young lady?'

'We … we have a ranch on Castle Creek, above Hill City, in the Black Hills.'

'What're you doin' in Cheyenne?'

'We brought a big bunch of steers to sell.'

He studied her hard for several seconds. 'So what are you gonna do now?'

Louellen took a deep breath, forcing her mind beyond the grief that engulfed it. 'I'll … I'll have to … to take Father home. Mother's a strong woman. We'll … we'll be able to… manage.'

The marshal pursed his lips. 'Well, takin' into account what you just did here, I don't doubt that a bit. I'm right sorry about your pa. You want me to get the undertaker?'

'Would you, please? Can I take him … I mean, will the stagecoach take him home with me?'

The marshal nodded. 'They can do that. The undertaker'll fix 'im up for it, an' they'll put 'im up on top. They do that, time to time. I 'spect they'll charge you for a ticket, same as if he was a passenger, but I don't rightly know.'

She took a deep, ragged breath. 'Where is the stage office?'

The woman Doug had rescued from the gunman spoke up. 'I am well acquainted here in Cheyenne. I will be more than happy to help you with the arrangements.' She held out a gloved hand. 'My name is Millicent Traverse. I don't believe I've heard your name.'

Louellen took the hand and returned its firm grip. 'I'm Louellen Kenyon. But folks just call me Red.'

'That's obviously quite appropriate,' Millicent observed, appraising the lush curls of red hair that cascaded down past Louellen's shoulders, her hat having fallen off during the fray.

'Millie'll take good care of ya,' the marshal offered his assurances. 'Her husband's a solid citizen o' Cheyenne. They're good folks.'

'Thank you,' Louellen offered, grateful for an unexpected friend in the middle of her horrific situation. Even so, she knew it was going to be a long way home.

Neither woman took note of the man who had come on a dead run, cursing under his breath, at the sound of the shots. He watched the pair walk away, muttering fierce words of self-reproach.

'Stupid!' he muttered, almost under his breath. 'I thought they'd be fine right here in town, just goin' from the hotel to a café. Right in Cheyenne. Right in the middle of a street.'

He watched Louellen and Millie walk away. His shoulders sagged as if the weight of the world had just settled on his shoulders.

CHAPTER 8

The sign above the door announced the establishment as the office of the Cheyenne and Blackhills Stage and Express Line. Louellen stood at the desk, her eyes puffy and red, but dry.

'Ma'am, I'm plumb sorry. I know you're in a tough situation. You sure got my sympathy. But we just can't do that.'

She frowned at the man's enormous moustache, as if it were the source of her irritation. 'You can't transport my father's body back to Hill City?'

'Oh, we can do that all right enough. That part ain't no problem. We can do it if the undertaker fixes 'im up in a casket or a rough box, either one. Or just wraps 'im in a tarp, for that matter, though that don't seem like it'd be fittin' for your pa, an' all. No, ma'am. That ain't the problem. It's the money we can't transport.'

'You can't haul money?'

'No, ma'am. Not on that run.'

'Why not?'

'Red Canyon's why not. Not to mention the Hat Crick Breaks. Then there's Robbers Roost a ways north o' Lusk. There ain't hardly a stage goes on the Cheyenne to Deadwood road that don't get held up somewhere along the way. Most likely in Red Canyon, if there's any amount o' money on it.'

'Really?' Louellen marveled. 'How would outlaws know what stage is hauling money?'

The agent shrugged. 'Danged if I know. Can't nobody else figger it out, neither. An' believe me, there's a passel o' lawmen tryin'. Even if we try to hide a strong-box someplace other'n up on top, they seem to know right where to look. So my orders is, until they figger out who's tippin' 'em off every time, we just ain't takin' no money shipments without a whole troop o' soldiers for an escort.

'Won't … won't the government provide an escort? Isn't that the army's job, to do things like that?'

'Not the way they see it. It takes a direct order from the governor or the president or someone like that, and that just ain't likely to happen.'

'Then why doesn't your company hire people to protect its own customers?'

'Well, the company's workin' on hirin' a dozen or so shotgun guards known for bein' quick on the trigger to put a stop to it, but that ain't happened yet, neither. So we just ain't haulin' no amounts o' money either way to or from Deadwood till further notice. Passengers is put on notice not to carry no more money than they want relieved of between here an' there.'

'There's nothing else you can do?'

'Not for now there ain't. I'm plumb sorry, but that's just the way it is. Rumor is that one company's makin' an armored coach that'll be bullet-proof, but that ain't happened yet, neither.'

Louellen fought to keep back the flood of tears that threatened. She had promised her father she would get the money from the cattle home to her mother. For a brief moment she considered doing it herself. That would entail buying a horse and saddle and carrying it with her the whole way. It was a long way.

It would be a long way by stage as well, but she would at least have the company, and probably the protection, of others. She would also be accompanying her father's body.

Her eyes were distant as she considered the road ahead of her. It was a three day trip at best. There was the road ranch by Fort Laramie where she could sleep inside, if the bedbugs didn't carry her away bodily before morning. The next one available that the stage stopped at was Jack Bowman's road ranch north of Hat Creek. It was the same story. Most of the stages just stopped wherever it became too dark to proceed, and allowed passengers to roll out bedrolls nearby or sleep sitting in the stage.

She forced her attention back to the agent. Try as she might, she couldn't keep the plaintive tone from her voice. 'Then what am I to do?'

The agent wiped his hand across his lower face as he scowled at the desk. When he looked up his eyes were soft, but his message didn't change. 'If'n you was my kid, I'd tell you to stick the money in a bank right here in Cheyenne. Then your own bank can figger out how to get it from here to there, or you can write drafts on it to whoever's willin' to accept a draft on a bank in some other place. Otherwise you could try to hire Boone May or one o' them fellas to escort ya, but they ain't likely to take on the job, neither.'

Louellen bit her lip. Had the agent known her well enough, he might have recognized the glint in her eye and questioned her further. He didn't. She had already discarded the man's clothing her father insisted she wear, and was most attractively attired. It might have been that in itself that prevented him from being at all suspicious of her intent.

'Well, then I guess that's what I'll have to do. I need to purchase a ticket to Hill City, then. For both me and my father, I guess.'

The agent took the money she offered and counted out her change. 'Stage leaves at five o'clock in the mornin'. Kin you have your stuff here, or do you need somebody to haul it over here from your hotel?'

'I ... I guess I'll need to have it hauled over here. It's more than I could carry.'

He nodded. 'I'll have Eddie over there with a buckboard for you an' your stuff about four-thirty then. Circumstances bein' what they are, I won't charge you nothin' for the extra service.'

'Thank you,' was all she could think to say.

'Gonna be the quietest three-day ride the Deadwood

stage ever had,' the agent mused, shaking his head as she left. 'There ain't none o' the usual passengers what'll know more'n six words to say with a real lady present. 'Specially one that purty.'

CHAPTER 9

Eddie, the flunky from the stage company, eyed the three large duffle bags sitting on the board sidewalk beside Louellen. 'All three o' them yours?' he demanded.

She shot a withering look at the lad. 'I don't remember any stipulations about how many clothes I am allowed to have,' she snapped.

'Most folks don't got but one,' he insisted.

'I am not most folks,' she retorted, making her voice as lofty as she was able. 'Besides, part of it is my father's.'

'Your pa's ridin' too? Where's he?'

She fought back the emotion that threatened to surge out of control. She channeled it into ire at the impudence of the flunky. 'If it were any of your business, I would inform you that my father was murdered two days ago, and it will be his body that will be riding atop the stagecoach as I'm taking him back home. Since it isn't any of your business, I won't bother to tell you that. Now do you have any more nosy questions about things that are none of your business, or may we proceed?'

Properly chagrined, the young man jerked off his hat and held it against his chest. 'Beggin' your pardon, ma'am. I … I didn't know nothin' 'bout that there. I … I'm plumb sorry 'bout your pa. Here. I'll help you up, then I'll grab your stuff.'

'I am quite capable of getting into a buckboard by myself,' she huffed.

More energetically than was required, she grabbed the edge of the buckboard, used the spokes of the wheel for steps and ascended to the seat, where she plopped down with much more emphasis than necessary.

The young fellow swallowed hard, jammed his hat back onto his head and loaded her three duffle bags into the conveyance. He grunted with mild surprise at their weight, but said nothing.

They rode to the stage station in total silence. As he pulled the team alongside the stagecoach she said, 'I would like my things loaded into the boot, rather than up on top,' she said. 'I don't want my clothes ruined with dust and rain.'

'Uh, yes, ma'am,' the still abashed youngster assented. 'Whatever you say.'

She watched carefully as he loaded them, assuring herself that they were well secured and fully shielded by the heavy leather cover.

'Did you have any trouble gettin' an account set up at the bank?'

She whirled to see the station agent looking at her appraisingly. 'No! No, it was no trouble. They were, uh, very accommodating,' she assured him.

He looked at her another long moment, then nodded his head once. He opened the door of the stagecoach for her, offering her his hand. Swallowing her irritation, she almost giggled at what she was thinking. She was angry because she was being treated like a lady!

She took the agent's hand and stepped up gingerly into the coach. She would never have admitted it, but she was grateful for his help. Aside from the large handbag she carried, she had a heavy wool blanket folded over one arm.

Three men were already seated in the stage. All three lifted their hats. Two of the three tried to mask their surprise that a young woman would be riding the coach. She wondered briefly at that, noting that there was already a woman, wearing considerable makeup, seated in the coach.

As she sat down, all three men replaced their hats. Two continued to look decidedly uncomfortable. The other smiled consolingly and said, 'I'm plumb sorry about your dad, Red.'

Startled, she looked at the man for the first time, and gasped. 'Shannon!' she exclaimed. 'How did you get here?'

'It's gonna be a long ride to Hill City.'

She sighed heavily. 'Yes.' Then her eyes opened wider. 'How did you know I'd be riding the stage to Hill City?'

Instead of answering her question he said again, 'I'm really sorry about your father. A man couldn't ask for a better neighbor. Or friend.'

She took a deep breath. 'It seems so unreal that Father is … is in the casket on top.'

The other two men and the woman spoke, but their words were unintelligible because they all spoke at once, all offering what she assumed were words of condolence.

As if desperate to find some semblance of normality in banal conversation, she said, 'I have gotten a lot better since you showed me how to aim my rifle with both eyes open.'

He nodded. 'Tryin' my best to be a good neighbor,' he offered. 'Your ma wasn't too fond of me for a long while. I didn't make a habit o' callin' at your house until she got to know me better. But your pa and I have been friends a long time.'

Louellen smiled tightly. 'You probably already know it, but Mother wasn't terribly happy the first time Father told her he'd invited you over for supper.'

Creed's voice betrayed the barest hint of a chuckle. 'Yeah, I'm the hard case your mother probably warned you about.'

Louellen colored instantly. 'Very emphatically, if you really want to know. But then the first time you didn't show up when we were expecting you, it was she who made Father ride clear over to your place to be sure you were OK.'

Creed chuckled. 'She finally accepted that the money I started out with was made with a gun, but it was honest money, and I was wearin' a badge. Sometimes duty manages to include a reward. That deal with the Broken Boot helped the most. Then I managed to put together a pretty decent bunch of strays I gathered up down along the Oregon Trail. It's surprising how many heads wander off and get lost when folks don't wanta take time to hunt for 'em. Or are afraid they'll get left behind if they do. The Indians eat a lot of 'em, but I managed to find a lot they didn't. A few of 'em even show bein' crossed with buffalo.'

'I know all that. I really didn't mean to insult you or … insinuate anything.'

When he didn't answer she brashly asked, 'Why are you riding the stage back from Cheyenne?'

He grinned. 'Now who's bein' nosy?'

She turned red again. 'I'm sorry.'

'Don't be,' he said quickly. 'I, uh, just sorta happened to be in Cheyenne. I … um, got offered a price I couldn't turn down for the horse I was ridin', so I decided I'd ride this buggy home.'

'Oh.'

After several minutes she realized there was a measure of discomfort beyond her presence weighing on them. Then it dawned on her. She had grown accustomed to being treated almost like any other hand on her parents' ranch. These men would have no idea how they were expected to behave in the company of a respectable woman during such a long trip.

'Feel free to go ahead and smoke or chew or whatever,' she said softly. 'It won't offend me in the least. I'm used to just being treated like one of the crew at home.'

Relief flowed through the stage like a fresh breeze. Just then the stage agent called to the driver. 'Head 'em out, Slim. That's all that's ridin' today.'

Almost instantly there was a loud crack of a whip and the gravelly voice of the driver yelling, 'Heyaah! Get a move on!'

The six horses leaned into their harnesses and the stage lurched forward. A grizzled old cowboy who must have been nearly fifty pulled out a bag of Bull Durham and a sheaf of papers and began rolling himself a cigarette. When he had it lit and the smoke drifted out the window, one of the others pulled out a slim cigar and lit up as well.

Louellen scarcely noticed. She mentally rehearsed where everything was in her duffle bags. Every pocket of every garment had money sewn into it, so it could not possibly fall out, even if a duffle bag came open. There was enough gold along with the paper money to make the bags heavy, but even if they were robbed, it was unlikely road agents would go through the passengers' clothing. *If they do, it will be over my dead body,* she ensured herself. *I am going to get that money back to Mother!*

CHAPTER 10

A deaf and blind barfly, filled to the gills with rotgut whisky, could have sensed the change in the passengers. Nobody announced they were entering Red Canyon. There were no road signs to mark the spot. It just seemed as if the wood, metal and leather of the big conveyance somehow imparted the information of its own accord.

The smell of dust in the air took on a sharp tang of danger. The shadows that hugged trees and brush seemed to assume a deeper, more ominous shade. Gullies that opened off the main canyon were suddenly deeper, more brush-choked than a hundred others just like them had appeared.

It was, after all, Red Canyon. It seemed as if even the six-horse team knew it. Every two-legged creature aboard certainly did.

Louellen was as bone-tired as the rest of the passengers had to be. The horses were replaced with a fresh team at the stage stations, roughly ten miles apart. The people were not so fortunate.

A day riding in a stagecoach is enough to convince most folks to never travel again. A longer trip, such as the normal run from Cheyenne to Deadwood, was three days at the minimum. That's if everything went well, if there were no broken wheels or axles, no flooded creeks or deep mud holes, and most of all, no holdups.

'The only other time I rode a stage through here we really lucked out,' Spud, the old-timer among the passengers said.

'You've been through here on the stage before?' the youth, Harvey, responded instantly.

The old cowboy turned his head and spat out the window. 'Yup. Once.'

'I can't imagine what would possess you to ride this thing twice,' Louellen offered.

The rest of the passengers chuckled appreciatively.

'So what happened when you rode it afore?' Creed asked.

'Lucked out, that's what happened. It was pert near a year ago. Like this year, I'd decided to head down to Cheyenne an' get rid of a year's worth o' wages,' Spud began.

'That wouldn't take long,' Harvey interjected. 'I couldn't believe what things cost in Cheyenne.'

'You're gonna find it a whole lot worse, once you get to Deadwood,' Shannon declared. 'Whatever anything cost you in Cheyenne, you can just about double it in Deadwood.'

Harvey's face paled perceptibly. 'Really? You ain't just puttin' me on, are ya?'

Dolly, the other woman among the passengers, spoke up, daring to enter the conversation for the first time. 'It's that way in any boom town,' she said. 'There are too many people coming in, looking for a mother-lode of tin, or for gold that everybody else has missed, so things are scarce. That always drives up the prices of everything.'

'Yeah, but it means there's plenty o' jobs for folks that wanta work, instead o' trampin' around through the hills, hopin' to get rich overnight.'

'I don't just want a job,' Harvey declared. 'I want to be one of the ones who strike it rich. I've heard if you walk down the right canyon, you can spot veins of tin ore, or even gold, sticking right out of the sides.'

Spud snorted. 'If ya could, there's a few thousand guys ahead of ya that already cleaned them veins out,' he growled. 'For every guy that finds enough paydirt to keep from starvin', there's a hundred or three that end up dead broke an' all but beggin' for a way to get their-selves back where they come from.'

Harvey swallowed visibly, staring at the old cowboy. Creed brought the conversation back to the present. 'So what happened comin' through here?' he asked again.

'Well, like I said, we lucked out. Sure 'nough, there was half a dozen fellas all set up to rob the stage. Happens on a right reg'lar basis. What they didn't figger on was a small bunch o' Sioux that was on a war party, figgerin' to attack the same stage. When the holdup fellas come ridin' hell-fer-leather outa the gully they was waitin' in, they pert near run over the war party o'

Indians what was hid out in the brush.'

'You have got to be kidding,' Dolly marveled.

'God's truth,' Spud declared, holding up a hand as if swearing an oath. 'O' course the Indians reacted quicker, an' started shootin' at the holdup guys. But they was purty quick too. They all bailed off their horses into the brush and started returnin' fire. Walt – our driver up there – was the same one drivin' the stage that day. He just hauled in the horses an' stopped dead still. Everyone on the stage grabbed a rifle, ducked behind whatever cover we could, an' got all set to fight off whoever was left to come after us.'

'Who won?' Harvey demanded, sounding almost breathless.

Spud looked at the youth as if he were about to break into laughter at his eagerness. 'Nobody, near as we could tell. They burnt up a bunch o' gunpowder an' busted a year's worth o' growth off the bushes. The Indians made a break first. They left one behind, an' had another that was havin' trouble hangin' onto his horse. The holdup guys went gallopin' off the other way, with two empty saddles an' a couple lookin' some wounded. They'd both had all the fight they wanted for one day. We went on through the canyon, all the way to Custer City, without no more trouble.'

Harvey frowned. 'Were the ones left behind dead?'

Spud spat out the window again. 'Danged if I know. Most likely, or the rest wouldn'ta left 'em.'

'You didn't go check on 'em?'

Spud studied the lad for a long moment. The

youngster paled beneath the stare, but held his ground, waiting for an answer. Finally Spud shook his head.

'Son, if you think any one of us was about to go pokin' around in them bushes to see if somebody was dead or just almost dead, you got another think comin'. We couldn'ta seen 'em till we was right on top of 'em, an' they woulda heard us comin', crashin' through the brush, from half a mile away. Nossiree. White or Indian didn't matter a whit, about then. They was on their own, if they wasn't dead already.'

'I shot a bobcat out of a tree once,' Louellen put in unexpectedly.

'What with?' Creed asked instantly.

'My pistol.'

'You shot a bobcat with your pistol?'

'Yeah. I thought I got him right in the head. He just tumbled out of the tree and landed with a crash in the brush.'

Silence seized the group as all eyes stared at Louellen, waiting for the rest of the story.

She showed the instinct of having been raised among cowboys, waiting just long enough to whet their anticipation, garnering their undivided attention.

'We walked over to pick him up. I was going to take him home to show my mother. And to horrify her, to be perfectly honest. But he wasn't there.'

'They're right hard to kill,' Spud offered.

'I wanted to look for him, but my father wouldn't let me. He made me hightail it out of the brush and back to our horses.'

'Smart man. That cat mighta been pert near dead, but you ain't gonna find me trompin' around in the bushes lookin' for 'im. Even if it was just a bobcat, they're fierce critters. An' bein' wounded, he'da been even worse.'

Louellen sighed heavily. 'I know it. I knew it then. I knew my father was right. But I just really, really hate to shoot something and not know it's dead. Even a bobcat.'

'Weren't you carrying a rifle?' Dolly demanded, her voice sounding almost accusatory.

Louellen colored slightly. 'Well, yes. We both had rifles with us. But it was close enough I was sure I could hit it with my pistol. I guess I thought I'd have more bragging rights when I showed it to my mother if I shot it with my pistol.'

'Stage station ahead,' the driver shouted, interrupting the conversation.

'Leg stretchin' time,' Spud declared. 'None too soon, either.'

As the team was replaced with a fresh team, the women walked together to the outhouse. Louellen said nothing, but she thought how strange it was that she and a woman she was sure was a saloon whore were walking together like two old friends.

In twenty minutes they were back in the less-than-comfortably cramped quarters of the stagecoach. Louellen wondered idly where they would stop for the night. She hoped it would be at a decent camp site, rather than a stage station. The ground was not that hard to sleep on, and she well knew all the stories of those who slept at the stage stations nearly being eaten alive by bedbugs. Then when she got home, she'd have to put all her clothes on the ground by a big ant hill and walk naked to the house behind a blanket her mother held in front of her, so she wouldn't bring bedbugs into the house.

Besides, if she were sleeping in her bedroll on the ground, she could position it where she could keep an eye on the stage, and be sure nobody was rummaging around among the baggage in the boot.

The sense of foreboding only increased as they left the stage station. They crossed the creek, and the fresh team picked up their pace in spite of climbing in elevation.

'We seem to be going faster,' Dolly observed.

'Walt'll push the horses for all they're worth till we get to the Beaver Crick station,' Spud informed her. 'Once we get past there, we got a better chance o' makin' it without gettin' held up.'

Dolly frowned and put into words what the others were thinking. 'If they know just about where the outlaws will hold up the stage, why don't they do something about it?'

'They're workin' on it,' Spud explained. 'The trouble is, they'd have to have a half dozen outriders at least the whole way from Cheyenne to Deadwood an' back again. They can't just have a good bunch o' fellas sittin' here in the middle o' Red Canyon all the time, just a-waitin' for the stage to come along, so they can escort it. An' hirin' that many men good enough to do the job would cost 'em an arm an' a leg. This here run ain't too profitable for 'em to begin with. If they did that, they'd be losin' money hand over fist.'

'So they just let us get robbed?' Harvey demanded, his voice shrill with umbrage.

'Well, they change up the schedule regular. That way the bad guys don't know what day we're a-comin', or what time o' day. That way they're in the same boat. If they wanta rob us, they gotta have some way o' knowin' when the stage is comin', or else just camp in the canyon an' wait.'

Creed put in his two cents worth. 'If they did that, their camp wouldn't be that difficult for a posse to find. They just about have to have somebody in Cheyenne that tips them off.'

'How could they do that?'

'That wouldn't be all that hard. Whenever the stage leaves Cheyenne, especially if it's gonna be carryin' a lot o' money, their lookout in Cheyenne can send a telegram to Custer City, or Hill City, or Deadwood, or wherever the others are, to let 'em know.'

'But wouldn't the telegraph operator know who was getting the telegram with that information?'

'Oh, I 'spect they got some sort o' code, instead o' sayin' the stage is leavin' today with lots o' money on board. It'd say something like "Mother's doing well today", if it's got money and is about to leave, or "Mother isn't doing well", if there's nothing on the stage worth robbing.'

'Now how would you know that?' Dolly demanded.

Shannon grinned. 'Well, it ain't coz I'm part o' the gang. That's just what Garth told me.'

'Who's Garth?'

'Garth Emerson. He's the marshal at Hill City.'

'Oh.'

Conversation waned as every passenger craned their necks to watch out the window, wondering if danger would erupt from one of the multitude of gullies and canyons opening off Red Canyon. They wouldn't have long to wait.

CHAPTER 11

'Trouble, folks!'

Walt's deep bass voice ignited a furor of activity within the stagecoach.

'What's up, Walt?' Spud called.

'Dead tree on the road up ahead,' Walt announced. 'Ain't no way to get around it, an' there ain't no way it just fell down there all by itself. Whoa, there!' he called to the team, hauling on the lines as he pulled on the brake lever. They came to a stop while still more than a hundred yards from the makeshift blockade of the road.

The stage station was more than two miles behind them. They had crossed the creek twice since leaving there. The Beaver Creek station was still seven or eight miles ahead. They were isolated.

Spud and Harvey followed Shannon's lead, picking up their rifles from where they leaned in a corner and jacking a shell into the chamber. Spud opened one door and Shannon the other. They slid out, crouching low, watching for any movement from the brush.

'Where you reckon they're at?' Spud asked quietly.

Walt and Lefty MacMillan, the shotgun guard, dropped down off the top of the stage. Walt held a rifle, while Lefty gripped his double-barreled twelve gauge shotgun, loaded with double-ought buckshot.

'Ain't spotted 'em yet.'

'You ladies best get down on the floor an' keep your heads down.'

Face aflame with anger, Louellen slid out of the door and shut it behind her. She gripped her bag, but appeared to have no weapon.

'Get back inside!' Creed ordered.

'You get back inside if you want to,' she retorted. 'I am not about to cower and hide from some low-life road agents.'

Creed studied her face with a mixture of irritation and admiration. He grinned suddenly. 'Red Kenyon, the hellcat o' Red Canyon, huh?'

She burned holes in Creed with her glare, but held her tongue.

'What're they waitin' for?' Harvey worried.

'Waitin' for us to decide they ain't there an' go over to move the tree outa the way.'

'We'll wait 'em out,' Walt decided. 'We're in better shape here, usin' the coach for cover, than we would be over there in the open.'

'They'll get impatient right shortly,' Spud ventured.

His words were no more spoken than a shot rang out from the brush, a hundred yards ahead and to the right of the road.

Using the slight wisp of smoke from the gunpowder to mark the spot, both Creed and Spud fired several rounds into the brush in response.

A bullet from the opposite side of the road kicked up dust at Walt's feet. He cursed and ducked as far behind the wheel of the stagecoach as he could, using the wheel to rest his rifle and try to see whomever had fired the shot.

'You folks had just as well throw down your guns,' a voice yelled from the brush. 'We got ya surrounded. We'll shoot the horses if need be, so you can't go nowhere. We can sit here an' pick you all off one at a time, if that's what you want. Or we can just take your money an' you folks can just go your merry way without nobody gettin' hurt.'

In spite of the anger boiling within every one of them, they all recognized the wisdom of the words. The robbers were in heavy cover. They were stopped dead on the road, with no place to run and no room to turn around. Even if they knew their exact position, getting a bullet to follow a straight path without being deflected by the brush would be almost impossible. The area immediately around the coach was devoid of cover. Nobody was going to be able to sneak into the brush and circle around them.

'We're sittin' ducks,' Lefty fretted.

''Fraid so,' Walt agreed.

'We ain't haulin' no strongbox,' Walt called out. 'The company won't let us carry no amount o' nothin' no more.'

'We'll settle for what the passengers is carryin',' the voice responded.

Louellen's eyes darted to the boot and back toward the voice. *Would they actually go through the baggage?*

The look was not lost on Creed. 'You got somethin' in your bags by chance, Red?' he demanded in a soft whisper.

'That's ... that's none of your business!' she whispered back.

'We ain't got no choice,' Walt said in a voice just loud enough for the passengers to hear. 'It's either throw down our guns or get gunned down.'

Nobody responded, because nobody could argue with the obvious truth of the statement.

After a long silence Walt called out, 'All right. I guess we ain't got no choice.'

He lowered the hammer on his rifle and threw it on the ground. He drew the pistol from its holster and tossed it down beside the rifle. One by one the others followed suit.

The voice in the brush said, 'Grab your horses, fellas. Let's go see what these nice folks brung us.'

Far back in the brush on both sides of the road bushes began to rustle and crackle. Three horses from each side became visible as they were led from the low gullies in which they had been hidden. The outlaws mounted. From each side of the road they approached the stage and fanned out in a large semi-circle. Each man held a rifle, some across their saddle, some with the butt of the stock resting on a leg, pointing up in the air.

Each man had a neckerchief covering the lower half of his face.

'Whoever's hidin' in the coach, open both doors an' get out here, with your hands in the air.'

A moment of heavy silence was followed by the rustling of petticoats as Dolly got up off the floor. She opened both doors then stepped out the same side as Louellen had exited, glaring daggers at the bandits.

'Leave the doors open,' the leader of the brigands ordered. 'I like to see right on through, just to be sorta careful.'

'Just as well to empty your pockets, folks,' the driver said, frustrated resignation heavy in his deep voice.

'Aw, don't mind the small change,' the leader of the gang grinned. 'We just want what's in the casket up there.'

Every face went blank in stunned surprise. All eyes jerked to Louellen of one accord, then swiveled up to the casket, roped down on top of the stage.

'What?' Walt demanded.

It was evident the leader of the outlaws was grinning behind his neckerchief. 'It seems the little lady has a whole bunch o' money from her an' her pa sellin' stock,' he announced. 'Her ol' man went an' got hisself kilt, so she's gotta do somethin' with the money. The stage line won't haul it, cause they figger the risk is a mite high. It seems there just might be some bad guys around that'd be willin' to take it off her hands.'

He paused for the appreciative chuckle elicited from his cohorts. His eyes focused on Louellen. 'She went an' told the agent she put the money in the bank, but nobody saw her takin' no money to no bank. So we sorta scratched our heads some, and figgered out what we'd do in her shoes. What'd be better'n haulin' her ol' man home in a casket, an' lettin' him be the one to tote all that money, right there in his casket with him.'

He turned his head to one of his gang. 'Skinny, climb up there an' open that there casket. Let's have a look-see what the ol' man's carryin' home.'

Aghast, each of the stage's occupants looked helplessly at each other. Each glanced at his guns, lying on the ground, and immediately dismissed any possibility of resistance.

One of the outlaws leaped from his horse, climbed a wheel and boosted himself up onto the top of the stage. He whipped a knife from its sheath at his belt and severed the ropes holding the casket in place. He felt around both ends of the casket until he found the release button. He pressed it and opened the casket wide.

The odor of formaldehyde wafted upward. The air felt as dead as the man within the coffin. As if somehow abashed in the presence of death, his voice was almost hushed. 'There ain't nothin' here but a dead guy.'

'It's gotta be there,' the leader insisted. 'Feel around. It's likely underneath 'im.'

With obvious reluctance the man complied. As he groped around, heaving the body back and forth within its confines to search, Louellen's face grew darker and darker. Creed moved over beside her and put an arm around her shoulders.

As he moved, the leader grabbed the butt of his pistol, then relaxed when he realized Shannon's action held no threat to him.

Skinny leaped down from the stage, leaving the lid of the casket wide open. 'There ain't nothin' in there. I felt around clear to the bottom. There ain't nothin' in there but the dead guy.'

Louellen could contain herself no longer. 'So whoever told you I didn't put the money in the bank was wrong. But on the word of some vile scoundrel, you dare to defile the sacred dead? What kind of base barbarian are you?'

Above the neckerchief the leader's face reddened perceptibly at the rebuke. His eyes appeared abnormally pale even though they were heavily shadowed by his hat brim and the bandanna on his face. Those eyes flashed, then narrowed.

'Sacred dead, huh?' he said.

He whipped out his pistol and fired a bullet into the casket. The thunk of it slamming into flesh within the coffin was unmistakable.

'Now the dead's not only sacred, but holey, too.'

Louellen gasped. 'Why, you filthy … bastard!' she said.

From her bag she whipped out a .41 Colt revolver, raised it to arm's length, and fired. The bullet just grazed the outlaw's forehead, sending his hat flying into the air. He yelped in pain and dropped his gun.

As if waiting for just such a diversion, every one of

the men leaped forward and grabbed a discarded gun and began firing.

Shannon's first shot ripped through the ear of a horse, sending him into a bucking frenzy that crashed into the other two near him, making it impossible for any of them to get in a decent shot.

On the other side of the stage, the roar of Lefty's shotgun not only emptied one of the outlaws' saddles, it caused the other two horses to prance and fight against the reins.

In the middle of the pandemonium the leader yelled, 'Let's get outa here!'

It seemed as if bullets were flying in all directions, but the bandits left only one man lying in the road. One of the others seemed to be having trouble staying on his horse, but the five galloped off at a right angle to the road, disappearing up a narrow gully.

Standing ramrod straight, holding her right arm extended to full length, Louellen sent the last of her bullets after the fleeing outlaws. She was rewarded with the squeal of a horse that leaped sideways, then bucked a couple times before its rider could get it back in pursuit of the others.

'Anybody hit?' Walt demanded.

He was the only one who seemed to have any thought for possible casualties. The other four men stood, watching Louellen in slack-jawed amazement.

It was Dolly who had the presence of mind to respond to the driver. 'I don't think so. I don't see anybody bleeding.'

'Well, now, that's a danged miracle if I ever saw one,' Walt answered. He turned to Louellen, his astonishment quickly turning to anger. 'What in blazes did you think you were doing, young lady?! Were you trying to get us all killed?'

'That … that vile… He just deliberately shot my dead father! He shot right into his casket! What did you expect me to do? Just stand here like some helpless … female?'

Shannon laughed aloud. After an instant's silence, several of the others did as well.

'You are sorta female, in case you hadn't noticed,' Shannon reminded her.

Her anger was only aggravated by the laughter. 'I am quite well aware of being female. I am not helpless. I will not stand idly by and let such … such ruffians desecrate the dead.'

'Yeah, I sorta noticed that.'

'Now what do we do?' Harvey pondered.

Walt scratched his head. 'Well, me'n Lefty'll get that casket closed down, an' get it tied again. Don't guess we can do nothin' 'bout that bullet hole in it. Beggin' your pardon, but it ain't really hurtin' your pa none. While we're a-doin that, the rest o' you boys can see if you can get that tree moved enough to let us get by it.'

Dolly turned to Louellen. 'I don't know about you, but I need to visit Mrs Murphy on the other side of those bushes.'

Louellen glanced around at the busyness of the men. She said, 'Me too, but I need to reload my gun first.'

She replaced the spent cartridges in her pistol with fresh ones from her bag. Then she nodded silently, and she and Dolly walked away together. She thought again how strange it was that the two of them acted like best friends, but if they met in town neither was likely to speak to the other.

By the time they returned, the stagecoach was ready to go. The sun sank ever lower toward what they all knew would be a moonless night. Unspoken amongst them was the certainty that they would never be able to make it to the Beaver Creek stage station before it became too dark to travel.

Would the gang of robbers regroup and attack again? If so, would they come shooting instead of just trying to rob them, this time?

There was little they could do but proceed, come what may.

The silence in the coach grew heavy. Everyone seemed equally loathe to break it. Louellen, especially, was too deep in her own thoughts to consider doing so.

The squeaks and groans of springs, wood and leather began to seem like voices from long ago echoing in her head. She stared vacantly, allowing her mind to drift. Scene after scene flashed through her mind, unbidden, all stirred, it seemed, by her need to use her gun.

She saw herself riding a calf when she was barely four years old. Her father's voice seemed to be calling in the rattle of the coach. 'Hang on to the hide on both sides an' just try to balance! Quit tryin' to stay on by brute force.'

The calf had quickly bucked her off anyway, but every time her father made her get back on she began to sense more and more of the rhythm of the animal, and she began to stay on a little longer.

Her mind slid forward several years.

'What d'ya think, Red? Think you can ride 'im?'

She was six then. Her father stood holding the reins of a Shetland pony. It bore no saddle, just the bridle whose reins her father gripped. She grabbed the horse's mane and scrambled onto his back, accepting the reins from him. Obeying some instinct she didn't even try to understand, she kicked the pony into a run. Even if he were just a pony, that horse could run! She felt free, wild, powerful, balanced on his back, her full head of red hair splaying out behind her like wild flames, the thrumming of the horse's hoofs on the ground matching the excited hammering of her heart. She didn't stop kicking him, urging him to greater speed, all the way down the lane to the main road and back again.

'Oh, Papa, I love him!' she had exclaimed, flinging herself from the horse's back into her father's arms. 'He can fly like the wind!'

In another year she was riding the regular ranch horses, perched like a cockle burr, impossible to dislodge from their backs.

She was seven when she had fired the .41 Colt the first time. She had been shooting the single-shot .22 rifle her father had bought her, and learned to hit a rabbit in the head with nearly every shot. The pistol was a whole different thing! Gripping it tightly with both hands, she squeezed the trigger. The gun roared and leaped in her hands. The end of the barrel whipped upward. The front sight made a bruise in the center of her forehead. Her father laughed at her!

Determined to do better, she was ready for the gun's recoil on the next shot. Even so, it jumped too much for her to hit the target. She learned quickly, though. She learned to shoot it as accurately as she had the small-bore rifle. He father had the saddle-maker in town make her a belt and holster just for the pistol, and she began to wear it everywhere. She regularly challenged one or another of her father's ranch hands to a shooting contest, and won far more than she lost.

She was ten the first time she was allowed to shoot her father's .45. It was too large for her small hands, but she knew what to expect. She noted with satisfaction the small smile of pride on her father's face when her very first shot with it hit the target.

She was eleven when her father bought her a lever action, Winchester .22 caliber rifle. Her father bought her one to replace the single-shot one she had always used. She loved its smooth action, remarkable accuracy, and the rapidity with which she could empty a full magazine of bullets, all while maintaining her aim at her target.

By the time she was twelve or thirteen, she was riding with her father on a regular basis, as if she were one of the ranch hands. Her lever action was replaced by a pump action, allowing her even greater speed of reloading without lowering the gun.

She had caught hints of the tension between her parents at times, the conflicting desires of her mother to teach her to be a proper lady and know all the skills of cooking and laundry and keeping house, and her father's desire for her to be able to handle any situation without help. She was never sure whether it was just because he felt strongly she should be able to do so, or because she was a stand-in for that son he never had.

It was somewhere about that age she figured out her mother couldn't have any more children after she was born. Knowing how much her father wanted a son, she felt alternately ashamed she wasn't a boy and fiercely determined that she would be everything that son could have been or die trying. Sometimes she resented him for being disappointed with her, even though he never gave her any indication that he was. Sometimes she resented her mother instead for insisting that she learn to be a lady. In sudden mood swings she couldn't understand, she was alternately overwhelmed with intense desire to discard the working clothes and look and act like the young woman she was becoming. Then she would feel as if she were somehow betraying her father by her secret thoughts.

She was sixteen when she shot a man. She hadn't killed him, but she felt as if she might just as well have. She and her father had stumbled onto a pair of men using a running iron to put their own brand on several of her father's calves. Her father had declared them under arrest, disarmed them, and prepared to take them into town to turn them over to the sheriff. She saw one of them sneaking a hideout gun from his back pocket. She yelled at her father as she jerked her own gun out of its holster. She fired without even thinking about what she was doing. In her haste she only grazed his arm, but it was enough to make him drop the gun and it saved her father's life. She didn't see it, but she learned later the pair were hanged in town. She was glad she hadn't seen it.

An endless parade of such scenes played their way across her memory as the stagecoach bounced and rocked. Now her father was dead. Until a couple drops of water dripped onto her hand she wasn't even aware of the tears that coursed their way down her face.

She swiped impatiently at them and took a deep breath. She wasn't aware anyone had noticed until Dolly said softly, 'It's a hard land, isn't it, honey?'

She swiped the back of her hand across her dripping nose in a most unladylike manner. She turned her head as if to look out the window while she composed herself. She looked back at the floor of the stage. She nodded her head. 'Yeah. Sometimes.'

A tide of gratitude welled up within her, not only at the unexpected solicitousness of the woman who certainly had her own stories of grief and loss to tell, but at the three men who were all much too engrossed in some minor conversation between themselves. They could have convinced any jury they hadn't noticed a single tear.

She shoved the memories forcibly down into the back of her mind and took another deep breath.

'Will they try again?' she asked, trying to direct the conversation to a less threatening subject.

'Count on it,' Spud declared.

They all knew he was right.

CHAPTER 12

A pistol shot carried on the breeze. Every head jerked up.

'A ways off,' Spud declared.

'Likely him.'

'That's the third shot.'

'Yup. You reckon he got all three?'

'My money's on him,' Walt said. 'I ain't never known 'im to miss.'

'I don't remember meeting him until a few months ago. Mother didn't want him around for a while, but then she decided he was OK. He visits pretty often, actually.'

'That's not too surprisin'. He does stick purty close to home, up there along Castle Creek, but it's not too far from you folks. You'd go by within a mile o' his place on your way to town.'

'I think he's our closest neighbor. Our place is right on up the creek a few miles.'

'Your pa knowed 'im well. He stayed away from your

place 'cause your ma pegged 'im as a gunman, an' didn't want 'im hangin' around. Your pa trusted 'im completely, though. That's why he didn't mind when Creed asked 'im if he'd like him to sorta keep an eye on you. He asked 'cause he didn't want your pa thinking he had any wrong intent, but you ridin' around the country alone all the time made 'im nervous.'

'He's been watching me because my father asked him to?!' Red demanded. 'Not because of … of … me?'

Spud chuckled. 'That's the way I heard it, but I 'spect he'd be payin' just as much attention to you if your pa hadn't asked him to.'

Her eyes widened suddenly. 'Was that why he was at that dance, that time, when he killed those guys?'

'Yup, most likely.'

Her eyes were wide, incredulous. 'That's why he was at that dance? He was there to keep tabs on me, and ended up needing to help Heidi?'

'Could be. Prob'ly not, though, now that I think about it. Your pa was with you, so he wouldn'ta been worried. Naw, he was most likely just there enjoyin' the entertainment an' plannin' on havin' a dance or two with you. I 'spect he just happened to notice them two wanderin' off where he didn't figger it was safe. He's sorta got a habit o' just bein' there when someone's in a bind. Happens often enough it gets a little spooky, to be right honest.'

There was almost a note of awe in her voice. 'Like some guardian angel, or something?'

Spud shrugged his shoulders. 'I ain't that

superstitious. Sorta makes ya wonder, though. I don't reckon your pa woulda been lettin' you wander off all over the country the past couple years the way he has if he hadn't known Creed was ridin' herd on ya.'

The mention of her father brought a dark pall over Louellen's mood that had lifted a little since their encounter with the gang of robbers. They were still a good five miles from the Beaver Creek stage station, in the upper reaches of Red Canyon. Just before it got too dark to see, they had stopped, unhitched the team and picketed them out on good grass, where they could easily reach the creek they had already crossed half a dozen times.

Somebody had gathered wood, and they had a cheerful fire going. Shannon had said, 'I'll see if I can scare up a rabbit or two for supper.'

'Pert near too dark to see 'em,' Spud conjectured.

'They don't run as quick thataway,' was all Creed had answered.

A few minutes later they heard his gun bark once. About ten minutes later it rang out again. The third shot was from farther away.

They neither saw nor heard him return. One minute they were all gathered around the fire. The next minute he was squatted among them, arranging three large cottontail rabbits on sticks to roast.

Thirty minutes later the three hapless animals were reduced to bones, tossed aside into the brush for the mice to seek out and chew on.

'Well, that was plenty o' meat for supper. Plenty o'

water in the crick. Couldn't ask for much more, I guess,' Lefty observed.

'Which one of ya was supposed to bring the biscuits an' blackberry jam?' Walt demanded.

'Wasn't that you, Dolly?' Louellen gibed.

Dolly actually smiled. As the firelight danced off her teeth, she said, 'My Dutch oven got too heavy before I got to the stage station. I traded it for this.'

From the large bag that lay beside her she withdrew a large bottle of whiskey. She removed the top and handed it to Walt. 'Pass it around.'

'Well now, somebody did remember to bring along the necessities of life!' Walt responded. Instead of taking a drink he handed it back to her. 'If I ain't mistaken, though, the one that brings the bottle always gets the first an' last drink.'

Dolly hesitated a brief moment before accepting the bottle back. She had deliberately not taken a drink first, lest any of the rest, certainly aware by now of her profession, would refuse to drink from the bottle after she did.

She tipped it up and took a big gulp, then passed it back to Walt. He swiped a hand across the mouth of the bottle out of habit, took a swig, and passed it on.

When it came to Shannon, seated on the ground next to Louellen, he took only a small sip. 'I'll pass on any bigger drink tonight,' he apologized, 'just in case them guys show up before daylight.'

As he said it, he cast a look all around the group, clearly urging them to caution as well.

'Here you go, Red,' Creed said, passing the bottle to

Louellen.

She took the bottle gingerly, feeling suddenly in a very difficult spot. She didn't really want to drink any of it. Her family had spoken disparagingly of any woman who drank, even though she knew a good many of them did privately. At the same time she didn't want anyone to get the idea she was haughty or snobbish.

She finally tipped the bottle and took a tiny sip, then hurriedly passed it on to Dolly. The liquid burned in her mouth, so she swallowed it quickly. Instead of being gone, it burned its way all the way down her esophagus, then seemed to spread its way around her stomach. By that time its burn was more of a glow than a searing burn though, she decided. Not at all unpleasant.

'You called me Red,' she accused Shannon.

He grinned at her. 'What else have I ever called you? Besides, did you forget you already told all of us that's what you usually get called?'

She laughed lightly. 'Actually, this trip is the first time I've been called by my name so many times in the last five years. Even my folks just call me "Red".'

'Red Kenyon, the Red Canyon hellcat,' Shannon tormented.

Before she could offer a retort Walt said, 'You'd best all get your blankets an' get 'em spread out where you wanta sleep. I'm gonna get rid o' this fire. I'd stay a little ways off the road, if I was you, just in case them guys come stumblin' along in the dark.'

'The moon'll be up a couple hours after midnight,' Spud said.

'As soon as it is, we'll get the team hitched up an' head out,' Walt said. 'The sooner we make it to the Beaver Creek station, the better I'll like it.'

Grabbing their blankets, the two women headed toward a patch of lush green grass Louellen had noticed before it got dark. She chose it because it was close enough to the stage to see the luggage boot in daylight, and close enough to hear anything going on there in the dark.

She pretended not to notice that Shannon had protectively spread his own blankets about as close as propriety permitted. The action pleased her more than she realized it would.

She must have slept. She was determined not to do so. She could sleep once they were on their way again, in spite of the stage's discomforts. Even so, it had been a very long and exhausting day.

She jerked awake as three gunshots rang out in the darkness. She grabbed her pistol as she jolted to a sitting position. In the darkness she could only make out dim suggestions of objects. She could hear nothing.

After a long moment Dolly whispered softly, 'Can you see anything?'

'No.'

'Is Shannon still there?'

'I don't know. I can't see anything. He must not be, though. He'd be moving if he was, after those shots.'

'Maybe it was him.'

A soft voice out of the darkness probed, 'You ladies all right?'

'Yes,' Louellen answered. 'Who's shooting?'

'Creed, I'm guessin'. He's the only one not accounted for.'

'It came from past where the horses is,' a whispered voice that sounded like Lefty guessed.

'Shall we go look?' Harvey's voice asked.

'Keep your voice down,' Walt scolded in a harsh whisper. 'No, we ain't goin' to go stumblin' along in the dark just to see where we can get shot.'

'Less than an hour before moonrise,' Spud's voice offered.

The whole group, awake now, crouched in the darkness together. They all jumped as another shadow suddenly joined them. 'They got three o' the horses,' Shannon said softly.

Walt swore. 'You get any of 'em?'

'Just one. Had to just shoot at sound, an' try not to hit a horse.'

'So we're down to three horses. There ain't no way three horses can pull a stage this heavy.'

'Somebody'll have to ride one of the horses we got left an' go for help.'

Silence settled on the group. It was Spud who said, 'How's about I rig up a hackamore with a hunk o' rope an' ride bareback to the Beaver Creek station? I can be pert near a mile up the road afore daylight. Then I can let 'im run. It'll be slower comin' back with a team, but we'll make good time, not pullin' nothin'. I should be back with a team an' a couple extra guns in three hours. Four tops.'

As if he'd already been thinking about it, Walt said, 'That blaze-faced sorrel's been ridden afore. He's the closest one to the stage, just off the road there.'

'I seen where you put 'im,' Spud answered.

'You might wanta walk alongside 'im, instead o' ridin', till you're a ways up the road,' Shannon suggested. 'Even in the dark you can get silhouetted against the sky an' offer 'em a good shot, if they're watchin'.'

Then Spud was simply gone. They heard only a few soft scuffing sounds, then there was nothing. The first thing that broke the silence was Louellen's voice.

'He gave me his rifle,' she said, sounding confused.

'Kinda hard to carry ridin' bareback in a hurry,' Walt explained. 'Besides, we might need it afore he gets back.'

'If he gets back,' Dolly unexpectedly said.

They all knew her words might well be prophetic.

CHAPTER 13

Silence settled softly across the darkness. Once they heard the chink of a hoof striking a rock a ways off, then nothing. Nobody spoke. Though each knew the others were all awake, no one was willing to speak and give away his or her position to whomever might be sneaking up on them.

An hour later the shadows softened perceptibly. Eyes that had been straining into the night and seeing nothing suddenly began to make out dim shapes.

The tip of the moon peeked above the hills to the east, as if it, too, were afraid to show itself too quickly. As the shining sphere slowly grew brazen enough to expose more and more of itself, it began to cast long shadows westerly of every rock, tree and bush. The broad canyon donned a mystical cloak of soft silver light.

By the time the full lunar orb braved its way above the hills, the land was bathed in its magical beauty. It spread the illusion of peace and safety, as the red soil, interspersed with the yellows and whites of clay hills and striated rocks took on their characteristic colors.

The illusion was shattered, just at the moment things became visible. A harsh voice shouted, 'Don't nobody move! We got all of ya spotted and covered. Where's the money?'

Walt responded immediately. 'We already done tol' ya. We ain't haulin' no money, no strongbox, nothin'. The stage line won't take no valuables on this run now.'

Louellen gripped the gun that was still covered by the blanket she sat on. She wondered if she were quick enough and accurate enough to shoot before she got shot. She knew she probably wasn't, but she wasn't about to divulge the location of all that money. She would die before she let it be lost!

Dolly stood up, moving toward the outlaw as she stood. She sighed so heavily it sounded almost melodramatic. She lifted her hands in a helpless gesture. 'It ain't worth gettin' us all killed over,' she said. 'I'll tell you where it is.'

The outlaw grinned and relaxed the slightest bit. Quick as a wink, Dolly stepped toward him. She swatted his gun upward with her left hand. His finger instinctively tightened on the trigger, firing into the air. At the same instant she lifted her knee into the man's groin with such vicious force it lifted his feet from the ground. He doubled forward in an irresistible paroxysm of pain, toppling over onto the ground, frozen in that curled position. He still gripped the gun, but was helpless to use it. Dolly stomped on the gun and the hand that held it several times. It was doubtful the pain of the broken fingers registered at the moment. It was equally doubt-ful his hand would respond to any effort to point or fire the gun for the time being.

As if it were a pre-arranged signal, so close behind the man's errant and involuntary firing of his gun, Creed's gun barked twice. Two other outlaws, who were confident they had everyone well covered, were distracted enough by Dolly's actions to give Shannon the split second he needed. Both men dropped to the ground.

Still doubled up on the ground, the man Dolly had kneed desperately fumbled with his left hand to get a hold of his gun. As he lifted it from the ground, Louellen's gun barked. The man grunted, looked at her disbelievingly, then collapsed.

Loud crashing in the brush on the opposite side of the stage betrayed the flight of the fourth and only sur-viving member of the group. Lefty's shotgun bellowed after him. Whether any of the shot actually reached him was irrelevant at that point. It was certain he would not be back.

'It was good of you to leave a couple of 'em for me at least, Red,' Creed offered with an exaggerated drawl.

Voices exploded from all sides of the stage as every-body suddenly tried to talk at once. When they subsided enough to distinguish what anyone was saying, Walt said, 'That there was the gutsiest thing I ever saw anyone do in my life!' he exclaimed. 'Dolly, remind me never to get on the wrong side o' you.'

The silence was suddenly oppressive. It was Dolly who

broke it. 'A woman in my line of work had better have a trick or two up her sleeve if she wants to live very long,' she said.

Another silence betrayed everyone's being at an unaccustomed loss for words. It was Louellen who finally said, 'I probably wouldn't have had to shoot him. I just felt like someone ought to put him out of his misery after Dolly was through with him.'

The words were met with far more laughter than they merited. When the silence once again seemed too heavy, Creed said, 'So what do we do now?'

Walt shrugged. 'I guess we'd just as well build a fire an' make some coffee.'

'Do we have a coffee pot?'

'Huh. No, I guess we don't. I guess we'd just as well get these fellas throwed up on top, so's we're ready when that other team gets here.'

Louellen stared fixedly at the body of the man she had shot. Dolly noticed. 'This trip is the first time you've ever actually shot at anyone, ain't it, honey?'

Louellen shook her head. 'No. It's the first time I ever killed anyone, though. Now I've killed two of them.'

She bit her lip. She knew if she tried to answer she would lose control and begin to cry again. She was not going to cry! She would rather die than let these people see her cry again.

She had been surprised at her own ability to react as swiftly and decisively as she had. Twice in the last twenty-four hours she had done so. Three times in the past week she had shot a man. Two of them she had killed. She had not thought about it ahead of time. She had only reacted, exactly as her father had taught her to do. He had taught her well. It was only after he was already dead that his teaching had been vindicated. He would never know what a good job he had done.

She bit her lip harder, hoping the pain would give her the control to keep from collapsing in tears. Dolly put an arm around her shoulders. 'It's all right, honey. Most women go all the way through life without ever having to do what you've had to do. You did good. Damn good!'

The shock of hearing a woman swear, so easily and so vehemently, helped. She gave a short laugh that was more sob than laugh. But she regained the control of her emotions.

'Let's go for a walk,' Dolly said.

She agreed readily. She really needed to walk a ways, besides needing to make use of the screening brush away from the men.

CHAPTER 14

'Spud's here.'

The small group looked at Shannon. As if by some unheard command, each head tilted sideways, yielding to the universal sense that it would somehow increase their hearing ability.

The rest heard the sounds almost at once. Several horses, trotting briskly, sounded a rhapsody more welcome than a trumpet fanfare would have been. Rescue was at hand!

Brisk activity kicked up small clouds of dust as things were put away, horses were led into position, and people readied themselves to climb back aboard the stranded conveyance.

A group of riders leading four extra horses rose into view as they topped a low hill in the road, then disappeared again as that road dipped down to cross the creek. They heard the splashing of water as the riders allowed the animals time to pause and drink. After a few minutes, they hove into view. Spud led the way, flanked by three other horsemen, trailing the four draft horses.

'Have any more trouble?' Spud called out.

'They tried again,' Walt said.

Spud looked around, clearly seeking any sign of casualties. 'Nobody hurt?'

Walt chuckled unexpectedly. 'Well now, one of 'em was hurtin' about as much as a man can hurt till Red went an' put 'im out of his misery.'

Spud frowned, clearly not satisfied with the answer. Instead of explaining, Walt said, 'They're all dead but one. I 'spect he's grabbed them three horses they got away with an' hightailed it by now.'

'Leader o' the bunch, I'm guessin',' Shannon said.

All eyes turned to him inquisitively, but nobody spoke for a long moment. It was Walt who asked, 'Why'd you say that?'

'The others came right out in plain sight. One stayed back in the brush where we couldn't see 'im, just in case the others didn't fare too well. My guess is that's the boss o' the outfit, lookin' out for himself, lettin' the others take the biggest risk.'

Silence gripped the group for a brief interval. 'Snaky cuss, huh?' Lefty observed.

Creed nodded. 'Which means he'll just gather up some more hard cases and keep on holdin' up stages or whatever else they're doin'.'

'You think he'll try again to rob us?' Louellen demanded, the fear obvious in her voice.

Creed shook his head. 'Not likely. He's too careful of

his own hide to try it by himself, and he isn't going to be able to put together another bunch that quick.'

He looked meaningfully at Louellen as he added, 'Whatever they were after on this stage will most likely make it.'

Louellen flushed a brilliant red, but she held her tongue.

In minutes, the horses were hitched and the stagecoach was moving again, flanked by the extra riders who had accompanied Spud. Clearly exhausted by spending the night getting to Custer City and back with the horses, he leaned back in a corner of the stage's seat and was soon snoring loudly, head tipped back, mouth open.

Louellen giggled at the sudden thought of what he would do if she reached over and dropped something in his mouth. Eyes twinkling, Creed said, 'I wouldn't, Red.'

Her eyes whipped to his. 'Wouldn't what?' she asked with feigned innocence.

Instead of answering, Shannon said, 'He spent a tough night while we was sleepin' nice an' peaceful. He deserves to sleep if he can in this thing.'

At the stage station in Custer City they ate a huge breakfast. Lefty, especially, regaled those who happened to also be at the table with details of their escapades. He embarrassed Louellen in particular by amplifying her role, making it sound as if she were some steely-nerved hellion single-handedly defying the whole outlaw gang. He used the term 'Red Kenyon, the Red Canyon hellcat' several times.

She constantly demurred, trying her best to counter his stories. Lefty was not to be denied, however. Aware he had the full attention of everyone, he piled it on more and more, describing exploits neither Daniel Boone nor Davy Crockett could have accomplished. Others soon joined in, enjoying Louellen's discomfiture and magnifying it with their effusive praise and adulation.

When she could stand it no longer, she rushed outside, stalking off toward the corral. Once there she had no idea what to do or where to go. She had to go back to the stage. She was sure that nobody would actually believe even half of the stories Lefty was relating. Well, some of it was true, she had to admit, but not at all the way he made it sound. Why was he embellishing everything so much?

'You know they're just teasing, don't you?'

The voice at her elbow startled her. She whirled and looked into the concerned eyes of Shannon Creed. She started to speak, then tears threatened to erupt, so she clamped her mouth shut instead. She took a deep breath.

Creed placed his forearms on a rail of the corral and leaned on them, staring at nothing on the other side of the barrier, silently waiting.

Her own voice sounded small and weak to herself as she asked, 'Why are they making fun of me? It's not at all funny!'

Creed turned to face her. She looked up into his eyes. 'I killed a man! It's not something to joke about!'

Her iron resolve abruptly melted. A small river of

103

tears coursed down her cheeks, threatening to wash away even the freckles. Creed reached out to her. She felt his arms wrap around her as if she were suddenly provided a haven from too many things she could not cope with all at once. She buried her face in his chest and surrendered to tears. The death of her father, her killing of his murderer, the frantic need to get the calf money home safely, the repeated confrontations with the outlaws, her killing of a second man, all rushed over her, threatening to sweep her away on a tide of emotion over which she suddenly had no control.

She flung her arms around Shannon and clung to him as if to a lifeline in a flood. She sobbed all of her fear and frustration in a torrent of words he couldn't begin to understand, pouring it all out as he simply held her, his face buried in the copious tangle of red hair, letting her just feel his presence and concern and draw whatever strength from it she might.

It was exactly what she needed. He offered no words of understanding, no advice, no efforts at consolation, no philosophical explanations of life at its hardest. He just held her, and waited.

When the reservoir of her stifled emotions had finally drained, she eased the tightness of her grip around him. He responded by loosening his own hold. With one hand he brushed the hair back from her face, wiping away some of the residue of tears from that cheek as he did.

She backed slightly away from him, hurriedly swiping the moisture from the other cheek. 'I ... I'm sorry!' she stammered. 'I'm acting like some weakling!'

He reached out and brushed at her hair again, leaving his hand on her shoulder. She lifted her red, swollen eyes upward until she was looking full into his. 'It's about time you let some of it out,' he said softly. 'You just can't hold it all in that long. That don't make you weak.'

'I'm acting like some ... woman!' she accused herself.

He chuckled. 'In case you hadn't noticed, you are a woman! An incredible woman, as a matter of fact.'

Her eyes darted to the stage station. Just on the outskirts of Custer City, it was known as one of the best places in town to eat. It was still early in the day, and breakfast customers were coming and going. Struggling to control her voice she said, 'I ... I don't want to go back in there.'

'There's no need to,' he said at once. 'It won't be long before the stage'll be ready to pull out. Let's just go ahead and get back in the stage and wait there.'

Grateful for the suggestion, she let him lead her to the stagecoach. Instead of sitting across from her as he had been, he sat beside her. It was fully half an hour before the others arrived and climbed back in. By that time she had regained her composure, and she and Creed were discussing how she and her mother could manage their ranch in her father's absence.

CHAPTER 15

The Cheyenne to Deadwood stage rolled into Hill City with more attention than usual.

Word of the escapades had preceded the convey-ance by several hours. Small clusters of people stood on the board sidewalks, watching the stage disgorge its passengers.

Shannon stepped down and turned at once, offering his hand to Louellen. She was already reaching for it, as if it were only natural he would do so. He steadied her as she stepped onto the ground.

Louellen's mother was waiting for her. With a stifled cry, she lunged for the open arms that beckoned to her. The two clung to each other in grief too deep for words for a long while.

After an amount of time deemed barely decent, several other people stepped forward. Offering Louellen a hand, a hug, a hand on the shoulder, each offered expressions of sympathy. So many! Before the gathered group thinned and drifted away, she was already wishing for solitude, for some escape from hearing the same words of condolence, the same expressions of emotion that always brought her tears anew.

Shannon stood back, watching, waiting. He well knew the money for which Louellen had paid so dearly was somewhere on that stage. He knew just as well that one of the outlaws had escaped, and was probably watching right now and he intended to make sure no attempt was made on that money here in town.

Eventually the crowd of well-wishers and sympathizers melted away. The two women suddenly found themselves alone beside the waiting stagecoach. When they had composed themselves sufficiently, the two women conferred quietly for a minute. Louellen approached Walt and spoke to him quietly.

His answer was not as quiet. He jerked his hat off his head and threw it forcefully onto the ground. He started to say something, pointing at Red. Then he stomped on his own hat, and swore. He pointed at her again.

'I knowed you'd pulled somethin' like that!' he accused her. 'You danged, knot-headed woman! You pert near got every one of us kilt, just cause you was too bull-headed to use the bank in Cheyenne. I don't know one reason on God's green earth why I oughta drive this stage over to the bank just to make it easy for you!'

Louellen flushed as red as her hair, but she remained silent. She simply looked imploringly at the grizzled veteran of too many narrow brushes with death. Finally he stooped over and picked up his hat from the dirt and dust of the street. He whipped it against his leg three times, knocking the bulk of the dirt from it. He studied it more carefully than necessary as he reshaped it, pushing in the right spots to bring the crown to a four-sided peak. He took a deep breath.

'Well, git on over here, then.'

As he climbed back up onto the stage, still grumbling profanities, Louellen and her mother hurried toward the bank. Creed still hung back, but followed on foot, keeping a lookout in all directions.

His eyes lit on a tall man lounging too casually against a post that supported the roof over the porch of the gunsmith's shop. His hat was pushed back from his head. The thatch of unkempt hair that moved in the breeze was so blond it was almost white. It failed to hide the raw gash at the top of his forehead, heavily scabbed over but clearly fresh. His pale blue eyes were cold and hard as he watched the two women. A Colt .45 was tied low on his right side. Another rode butt forward from the left side of his belt. Just behind it he wore a large Bowie knife.

Something in the man sent chills down Creed's back. As he followed the stage he kept making sidelong glances at the gunman. He thought the man had worked on the X K Bar several years ago, but didn't remember seeing him around since. Then he remembered he was one of those bested by Louellen in the shooting contest in town. The man's icy glare remained fixed on the two women until they walked into the bank. Only then did he turn and saunter next door, disappearing into one of the plentiful saloons along Hill City's main street.

By the time the stage reached the bank, the two women were coming back out of its door, accompanied by two bank employees, each carrying a large carpetbag. At Louellen's request, Walt opened the boot on the back of the stage.

It took the better part of half an hour for the women to go through her luggage, undoing the stitching of all the pockets and pouches holding the hidden treasure. By the time they were finished, both of the bank employees' bags were nearly full. The two men lifted them with an effort and carried them into the bank.

When the first of those hidden pockets was opened, Walt swore emphatically. He spat a brown stream into the dirt of the street. He glared holes through the young woman who studiously ignored him. When they indicated they were finished, he said, 'Now is it all right with you if I take your father's body on over to the undertaker, or do you have a bunch o' money sewed into his trousers too?'

He already knew the answer he didn't wait for. He climbed up onto the driver's seat and bellowed at the team. They left in haste enough to deliberately cover the two women with dust.

Once they and the money were safely inside the bank, Shannon heaved a great sigh of relief. He looked around for the blond gunman, but he was nowhere to be seen.

The funeral was held at the ranch two days later. It seemed that half the country must have come for it. Doug was well liked and universally respected. He was laid to rest in the small cemetery on the hill above the house.

For much of that day Louellen had sought out Shannon's company repeatedly. Mostly she just chatted idly, just wanting escape from the steady stream of condolences that always hurt more than helped. Only the day-to-day urgency of running a ranch began to dull the ache that weighed against the natural buoyancy of her personality.

CHAPTER 16

Louellen's heartbeat surged suddenly. Something caught at her throat, almost making her gasp. Suddenly short of breath, her head whipped around, this way and that. There was no explanation.

She was so tired! Her back and rump ached. Her knees and ankles sent regular demands for rest every time the horse's gait changed. She wanted only to get home, take care of her horse, eat something, and collapse into bed. Another half hour later and she should be there.

Louellen probably shouldn't have left the rest of the crew when she did. She had promised both her mother and Shannon she wouldn't strike out alone. It was a promise she had made reluctantly, and with little intention to be too careful in keeping it.

It had been a hard day for the whole crew. Separating calves from the cows to wean them was always a challenge, and demanded the very best from both horses and riders. They had started with the first rays of dawn, and finished past mid-afternoon. When the two bunches were separated by enough distance, half the crew stayed with each bunch to drive them to the separate pastures. That would make it relatively easy for one or two men with each bunch to prevent them from trying to reunite. After a week or so, the intensity of their desire to do so would ebb. Both bunches would begin to fatten up on the abundant grass. When it was time, the calves would be taken to sell, probably in Deadwood. That was a fairly easy day's drive, and provided an always hungry market that offered top dollar. She knew they weren't going to try another drive all the way to Cheyenne. Oh well. Time enough to worry about that when these calves were a year or a year-and-a-half old.

She should have waited another hour or so when the rest of the crew would also head for the ranch. A couple of hands would be back first thing in the morning to replace those staying all night. They would take over the duty of discouraging the weaning calves from searching for their mothers. For now the night hawks would have a fairly easy time of it. The calves were tired. They would graze a while, then lay down for the night.

She was simply too tired to wait that extra hour. Running a ranch was so much more work than she had imagined. Her father had always done things with such ease that it seemed almost as if the place ran itself. In the time since his funeral, she had quickly learned how wrong that impression was!

She was riding almost half asleep, content to let her horse pick the route and pace home. She knew the mare was just as eager as she for food and rest.

Then the animal's ears shot forward. Her gait hesitated slightly. Her head swung toward a neck of timber that extended to within 300 yards of the direction of Louellen's travel.

That didn't explain her reaction. The horse could have sensed a mountain lion, a coyote, another horse, almost anything. None of those things should have caused the icy fingers that unexpectedly shot down her spine. She was suddenly, almost mindlessly afraid. She fought an almost insurmountable urge to jam the horse's sides with her spurs and run. But from what? Why?

'What is it, Freckles?' she asked.

The oddly marked mare provided no explanation. It was easy to see where Louellen had gotten the name for her favorite mare. She was white, but her entire body was covered with small, perfectly round black dots, spaced several inches apart. She had never seen a horse with those markings before, and Freckles was the only conceivable name.

Freckles turned back away from whatever had arrested her attention, intent once again on heading for the welcome rest and feed waiting in the distant barn. The sense of danger did not leave Louellen as easily.

The western sun cast long shadows on the shaded side of every irregularity in the terrain, whether botanical or geological. There was almost no wind. A bald eagle hung motionless in some invisible thermal, watching with its phenomenal vision for some prey to move.

Abruptly the great bird folded its wings to its body and pointed downward, traveling with increasing speed toward the ground. Just when it seemed as if it must smash into the earth it spread its wings. A hapless rabbit was pounded with steel-hard talons, killed instantly by the force of the blow. In the same sweeping motion those talons dug into the soft flesh. Skimming over the ground the eagle began to beat its wings, swiftly soaring upward and away, the meal for a pair of eaglets in a distant nest held securely.

It should have been a scene of utter tranquility, buoyed by a sense of satisfaction for a hard day's work well done. Instead, Louellen felt as if she were the rabbit, just on the cusp of her own destruction. She actually glanced skyward, as if expecting to see another great avian diving toward her.

Her eyes followed the direction of the horse's brief attention, fixing on the tip of that neck of timber. She frowned. Nothing moved there. It was all in shadow from the sun, low in the sky as it was, but she could make out no movement.

Had she been able to penetrate the near darkness of the timber, she would have been even more terrified. A pair of preternaturally pale eyes watched from the cover of those trees. The face below the eyes was as expressionless as the eyes themselves. Had she been able to see them, both would have transmitted the same aura of a serpent watching a mouse that was soon to be its own supper. Neither had the least hint of any human emotion.

Torn between impatience at her own irrational fear and reminders of a hundred times her father had admonished her to always trust her horse's instincts, she touched her spurs lightly to the mare's sides.

The mare didn't really need much nudging. Aside from her own inexplicable unease with whatever was in the trees, there was the barn that beckoned from beyond the next ridge. She broke into a brisk trot with no further urging.

Louellen glanced over her shoulder every thirty seconds or so. She wasn't sure what she expected to see. She knew what she wanted to see behind her. Nothing. Nobody.

As if her haste was itself an impetus for greater fear, she nudged the horse again. The mare willingly lifted into a long lope, the rocks and brush around them slipping quickly past.

Her heart hammered. Her breath caught in her throat. An almost silent sob broke through her lips. She whipped her head around, looking in all directions. There was absolutely no reason apparent for her panic.

Shame suddenly overcame the irrational fear. She was a grown woman! She was the one responsible for running this ranch now. She was the one who had killed her father's murderer. She had helped fight off the outlaws that tried twice to rob the stage and take all the money from the sale of her cattle. She was armed, with both pistol and rifle. Who or what was she so afraid of?

Without realizing she was doing so, she dropped her hand to the .41 Colt holstered butt forward on her left side. She fingered the strap that held it in place, tempted to unbutton the strap so she could draw the weapon swiftly.

Instantly she demanded of herself, 'Draw it to do what? There's nobody there! There's nothing to shoot. What in the world is the matter with me?'

Even as she argued with herself she tugged on the reins, slowing the mare from a gallop to a swift trot. She should slow her even further. She had done a long, hard day's work. She deserved to at least go the rest of the way home without being further fatigued.

She couldn't bring herself to do so. Still glancing back over her shoulder every little ways, she continued the fast trot until she entered the X K Bar ranch yard. Only when Floris Van Der Hagen stepped out of the barn and walked to meet her did she rinse herself of that mindless sense of impending doom.

'In a bit of a hurry, are you, Red?' he called to her.

She bit her lip. She wasn't about to admit to the fear that had held her in its grip the last three miles. 'Oh, just letting Freckles have her head. She seems anxious to get to the barn tonight.'

'She looks like she's had a hard day, all right.'

'We both have.'

'Would you like for me to rub her down and put her away for you?'

'Oh, Van, that would be so nice of you! Would you mind?'

'Not at all, Red. That'll make up a little bit for me bein' the one left to idle around here, mindin' the place while the rest of you were out there working your hind ends off all day.'

She stepped down and handed the cowboy the reins. As he led the horse to the waiting barn, she hurried to the house. The nagging sense of being watched, of being in danger, of some imponderable threat hovering over her, left her only when she was inside the house.

CHAPTER 17

'Mr Creed, please don't turn around.'

If the voice had not been soft and feminine, Shannon would have reacted far differently. As it was, he froze with his hand on his gun. His mind raced. If it were someone wanting to kill or harm him, he wouldn't have been warned in advance. In fact, if it were someone wanting to kill him, it would have been a bullet that sped from that space between two buildings instead of a quiet voice.

'I have something that you need to know,' the voice continued.

Something in the voice was very familiar. He loosened his hold on his gun butt and wiped his hand across the holster, then scratched his ear, making what must have been an almost comical effort to appear casual.

He pulled a thin cigar from his shirt pocket, fished a match from a different pocket, leaned back against the corner of the building and lit the cigar. His response issued from his mouth within the small cloud of smoke.

'I'm listenin'.'

'You and Louellen are both in great danger,' the voice said.

The voice clicked in Creed's mind. 'Dolly? Is that you?'

'Shhh!' she cautioned. 'Don't use my name.'

'Sorry. I just recognized the voice and it surprised me. What's goin' on?'

'There's a man that I think was involved in trying to rob the stage. He hangs out in the saloon where I work quite a bit.'

'The Sundown Saloon?'

'How did you know that? I don't remember seeing you there.'

'I just snooped around a little after we got here. There's some o' the saloons that treat their workin' girls awful bad. I got no business makin' any judgments about how you make a livin', but after everything you did for Red on the way here I wanted to make sure you weren't in a bad situation.'

There was dead silence for a long moment. It almost sounded like her voice was about to crack with emotion when she finally responded. 'Why, Mr Creed! That's ... that's ... I don't know what to say. I'm ... well, I'm not used to anyone caring what happens to me. I'm ... it's...' She cleared her voice and took a deep breath. Her voice softer still she added, 'Alger Smeed runs the Sundown. He treats us fair. We have the right to refuse anyone we don't want to ... uh, do business with. For a working girl, it's not a bad place. I knew him in Cheyenne. That's why

119

I came to Hill City. It's hard to find a decent place to …'
She giggled unexpectedly, then continued her sentence.
'… a decent place to be in an indecent business.'

Creed smiled. 'Even if your business is indecent, you
are a decent person, Dolly. In fact, you're a good person.
I like you.'

'Be careful!' she cautioned.

'I'm serious. I'd be proud to be seen talking with you
anywhere. You don't have to sneak around to be sure
nobody notices.'

'I wouldn't take a chance on hurting your reputation.'

'Don't worry about that. I'm not all that high on most
folks' list of saints anyway, in case you hadn't noticed.'

She giggled softly again. 'So we actually have something in common, huh?'

Instead of answering he said, 'So what's this about
Red being in danger?'

Dolly took a deep breath. 'There's one guy that
hangs out at the Sundown quite a lot. I can't be sure, but
I think he was one of the outlaws that tried to rob the
stage. He has really weird eyes. They're almost creepy.'

'Mortenson.'

'You know him?'

'I know who he is. And I think you're right.'

'I haven't been able to hear anything absolute, but
he's really, really mad at somebody. He's been doing a
lot of awfully serious talking with three or four other
guys, but every time I work my way close enough to
maybe hear what they're talking about, they shut up. I
have heard him mention "that redhead" several times,

120

though. And he mentions your name in the same way. The way he says them sounds like you and her are both swear words.'

'That ain't too surprising. Both of us sorta messed up what he thought was gonna be a really big haul. That dumb kid had enough money stashed on the stage to keep him and his gang in whiskey and women for a year. Uh, beggin' your pardon. No offense meant.'

'None taken. You're right. But he's planning something else to get even.'

'Do you know what?'

'No! That's the problem. Like I said, every time I get close enough to maybe hear something, he gives a little wag with his finger and everybody shuts up. They obviously figure that since I was on that stage, I might let you know anything I learn.'

'Well, I don't guess I can do much about it except watch my back.'

'It's Red I'm more worried about. Or her mother.'

'Her mother?'

'It would be just like him to do something to her to get even with Red.'

Shannon felt his heart sink into the bottom of his stomach. He took a pull on the small cigar and slowly exhaled, thinking furiously. 'That scares me to death. You're right. That's exactly like something he'd do.'

'But what can you do?'

As if talking to himself, Creed said, 'I can let Flint know the danger. Red almost always rides with the crew when they go out to work cattle or anything. I've been spending quite a bit of time hanging back out of sight, making sure she don't take off somewhere alone.'

The soft giggle came again. 'She'd be furious if she knew you're doing that.'

'Yeah, she would. She's got more guts than brains sometimes.'

'But what about her mother?'

'I can ask Flint to be sure at least one hand stays at the place and keeps an eye peeled whenever the rest are gone. One man, with both a pistol and a shotgun, can be pretty good insurance. Especially if he keeps mostly out of sight and pays attention, so anybody riding in with something on their mind wouldn't even notice him.'

'Oh, that would ease my mind so much!'

'Other than that, I don't know what I can do except watch and wait. I'll just have to see what he's got up his sleeve, and hope I can react quick enough when he shows his hand.'

'Thank you.'

'If you do hear anything more, can you find a way to let me know?'

'I'm talking to you now, ain't I?'

As he tossed the small cigar down and ground it under his boot, the knot in Shannon's stomach did not ease a bit. He was positive Dolly was right. He was just as positive he would find out what the outlaw was planning. Even then he didn't understand how diabolical the man with the empty eyes could be.

CHAPTER 18

'I'm not sure we could be doing as well as we seem to be, without him.'

Louellen's eyes flashed. Her jaw muscles bunched. Her lower jaw thrust forward slightly. 'We do not need him riding herd on us like we're ... like we're...'

'Like we're a couple of women, trying to do a job most men couldn't do?' Xania challenged.

'We have an excellent foreman. Flint is as capable as anyone.'

Xania nodded her head. 'He is that, and he's as loyal as any man could be. These past couple of months would have been impossible without him. At the same time, Shannon's help and his suggestions have been even more helpful. He knows how to run a ranch. I don't know what we'd do without him. In fact, sometimes I worry that he's neglecting his own place to be over here as much as he is.'

Louellen took a deep breath. 'Do you know he's actually spying on us?'

Xania's eyebrows shot up. She opened and closed her mouth twice, then closed it again. Her voice carried all the offense of a cat that had been tossed into a stock tank. 'What on earth are you talking about? Why would he need to spy on us? How is he even doing it?'

Louellen met her mother's glare. 'Maybe not spying, but that's what it amounts to.'

'What on earth are you talking about?'

'I've spotted him three different times, staying way off to one side where he thought I wouldn't notice, just watching. I'm sure he's just shadowing me, in case I need help.'

'If that's the case, why doesn't he ride with you?'

'Because he thinks it'd make me mad if I thought he was … was …' She giggled. 'If I thought he was mothering me.'

'And does it make you mad?'

'A little. But at the same time it makes me feel safe. But that's not the only way he's spying on me.'

'How else?'

'Little Earl.'

'Flint and Hilda's boy?'

'Yes.'

'How is he spying on us?'

'He just told me that he's supposed to keep his eyes open, and if he sees something that he thinks we need help real bad with, he's to ride hell-for-leather to Shannon's and fetch him.'

Xania stood mouth agape for a long moment. She giggled then. 'I can't quite imagine Little Earl getting away with using the term "hell-for-leather".'

'I'm sure he couldn't, if either of his folks heard him. I think he was quoting Shannon.'

'You think Shannon told him that?'

'That's what he told me. He kept looking all around while he told me about it, and talking real quiet, like it was some big dark secret that he wasn't supposed to say anything about, but it made him feel so important he couldn't keep it to himself. It was like he was telling me he was helping "take care" of me.'

Xania giggled again. 'That's hilarious. And I can see Shannon doing exactly that. Not so much to keep tabs on anything we're doing, but to make a 10-year-old boy feel really big and important. I wonder if Flint knows.'

'I doubt it. Little Earl told me he wasn't supposed to tell anyone, not even his dad. But he said he thought I'd "rest easier" if I knew he was "looking after me".'

Xania giggled again. 'That's just so like Shannon. He makes both Little Earl and Bubbles feel so grown up.'

'Her name is Hildegarde. I don't like everyone calling her Bubbles.'

It seemed as if everything Louellen said made her mother giggle. 'How could she be called anything else, after what she did.'

'I don't think it's funny.'

'Oh, it is, though! I think it's one of the funniest thing I ever heard of. Here she is, all of eight years old … too young to even start to develop, but she thought she was. And who should she want to notice the fact but Shannon. So right in front of everyone she walked up to him, stretched her shirt tight across her chest, and announced to him, and to everyone on the place at the same time, "Look, Mr Creed! I'm starting to get bubbles already!"

'I have to admit, the only one that didn't nearly swallow his tongue was Shannon. He just pretended to take a look and said, "By Jing, you're gonna be a full-grown woman before you know it," like it was as normal as her showing him a new pair of shoes.

'And being a bunch of cowboys, there's no way her name is going to be anything other than Bubbles from now till kingdom come.'

'Poor kid.'

'There are worse things.'

'I still think it's terrible.'

'That doesn't tell me a thing about why it bothers you that he has Little Erland watching for you to need anything.'

Louellen's jaw set. 'Mother, I spend twelve to fifteen hours in the saddle every day, just like the rest of the hands. I keep track of every head of stock we have. I don't wait for Erland to make the decisions about where we move which bunch when they need fresh pasture. I ask his advice, but I make the decisions. I think I … we … are running the ranch every bit as well as Father did. And see, I even called him Erland like Father always did. Father said that was important to reinforce his status as foreman with the rest of the crew, so I do the same.'

Xania's eyes grew distant. A veil drew across them. She took in a large breath and exhaled it slowly.

'We're getting by. I admit that. But you can't keep up the pace. You're wearing yourself to a frazzle and worrying yourself into an early grave. Your father did all those things like it was second nature to him. I guess it probably was. We have to do them all very deliberately, mulling over every decision from all directions, then second-guessing ourselves.

'Should we put these bulls with the heifers or with the older stock? Should we put the main herd on the Peacepipe Valley grass, or save that for winter forage? Should we keep that bull that's always fighting with the others or trade him for a different one? That yellow piebald cow is the biggest pain in the herd when we're working cows, but she always throws the best calf we get. Is she worth the trouble she causes?'

It was Louellen's turn to issue a heavy sigh. 'I know, but we get the decisions made, and I think we're handling all the concerns we need to.'

Had she only known, those were lesser concerns than the ones she was about to confront.

CHAPTER 19

The trail was easy to follow. The fact that it was far too easy never occurred to her.

Louellen's blood boiled. It wasn't enough that her father had been shot down in cold blood. It obviously didn't matter to somebody that she and her mother were left to try to manage a ranch they weren't capable of managing. It didn't matter that the ranch hands were all busy at the other end of the ranch. Or maybe it did matter. Maybe that's exactly why they had chosen this time and place. By the time she could get to the crew, then get back to the trail, it would be too cold to follow, or else the rustlers would have time to dispose of the stolen stock.

That meant, in a nutshell, that it was up to her. OK, fine. Then she would take care of this too. A sense of wishing Shannon Creed was at her side washed over her. He had been especially attentive over the past months. She remembered back when her mother was so reluctant to make him welcome, but he had won her over. He had also spent a lot of time coaching Louellen in details of self-defense.

The biggest thing he had persuaded her to change was to move the pistol she carried to her left side, butt forward, at waist level. At first she had argued. She wanted him to teach her a fast draw, so she could match one of the outlaws if she needed to do so.

He had adamantly refused. The last thing he wanted was for her to get the idea she could go against a gunman in a stand-up gunfight. She was feisty. She was tough. He didn't want her to let those two realities foster her untimely demise.

She had reluctantly agreed, and made the switch. It had done nothing to damp the seething rage she felt at the events of the past months. She refused to allow those tragedies to cow her. She would not let the theft of a bunch of their best heifers cow her either. Nor would she waste the time it would take to go for help. She would forge ahead and take care of this with the same fury with which she had plunged into the role of running a ranch. She had done so with a fierce determination in the weeks following her father's funeral.

At least the money was in the bank in Hill City. So the stage driver and guard were still mad at her for sneaking it aboard the stage. Big whoop! Let them be as mad as they wanted to be. They'd either get over it eventually or stay mad a long time. It was no skin off her nose either way.

At least their money was safe. She still had no idea how the outlaws knew she had the money with her on the stage, but thanks to her and several other people they didn't get it. All but one of them was dead.

But now this! Blatantly, as if deliberately taunting her, a herd of twenty-five or twenty-six bred heifers had been gathered up and driven off. Rather than taking them north, toward the booming demand of Deadwood, they were driven south. That made no sense. Neither did it make sense that they made no effort to hide their trail!

The boldness of the theft angered her just as much as the theft itself. It was clearly a statement that the rustlers knew there was 'just that slip of a girl' to do anything about it, so they didn't even need ordinary precautions. That meant they knew where the rest of her crew was, which, in turn, meant they had been watching her or the ranch or both. The icecold fingers down her spine reminded her how many times she had felt watched.

Her mother's protests didn't help her disposition. She at least had the presence of mind to stop at the house and get her bedroll and supplies, in spite of her urge to just follow the trail immediately. That meant she'd had to explain to her mother where she was going and why. Then she had to face all the arguments, even demands, that she report it to the sheriff and leave it up to the law. She wasn't used to defying her mother, but she knew what would happen if she relied on the law. Nothing.

Well 'nothing' was simply not what was going to happen. She was going to find the thieves, drive them off, shoot them, or arrest them. Then she'd take the heifers home again. She'd show them a thing or two!

At Spring Creek she gained some ground. The

rustlers had clearly allowed the heifers time to drink and rest a while before they began to push them on southward. Because a single horse and rider could go considerably faster than even a small herd of cows, she had already gained a great deal. Even so she knew she wouldn't catch up with them before dark. She fumed inwardly at the reality, but resigned herself to it.

Near the head of French Creek she found a good spot to stop for the night. She picketed her horse, made a small fire, ate supper, and rolled into her blankets.

She was up again as the sun bathed the land in soft ambient light but before it showed its face. She made coffee, fried herself some bacon to grease the dry biscuits she had brought. Too impatient to chew them long enough, she began to dunk them in her coffee to soften them. The bacon grease and coffee didn't mix well. She grimaced as she ate, but gobbled them hurriedly anyway. She'd need the strength of the food. She didn't need to enjoy it.

She swiftly packed away her things, rolled her blankets, saddled her horse and returned to the trail left by the cattle thieves.

Those she pursued had stopped for the night along French Creek too! She found their campsite three miles downstream from where she had camped. She guessed she couldn't be more than that distance behind them.

Qualms cramped her stomach as she realized how close they were. She had watched the tracks and guessed there were four of them. Four to one wasn't great odds. Well, she'd just have to find a way to even the odds somehow when she caught up to them.

Maybe she could gallop into Custer City and ask the sheriff for help. She could make it there from here in a couple of hours. If she allowed for an hour there, then two hours back to pick up the trail again, they could still catch up to the cattle by dark.

That was provided the sheriff was in Custer City instead of out pursuing his duties elsewhere. And provided he was willing to do as she asked and able to assemble a quick posse. If he wasn't there, or wasn't willing to cooperate, she'd lose at least half a day and be no better off than she was already.

Reality niggled at the corners of her mind, whispering that she was terminally stupid to be pursuing four outlaws by herself. Fleeting images of the things that might happen to her flitted across her mind. She angrily thrust them aside.

Ahead, clearly in a direct line with the direction the stolen cattle were being driven, a great rift in the ridge of hills loomed. It looked as if a giant knife had sliced a wedge out of the low mountains and carried it off to use elsewhere. The result was a narrow defile that sloped steeply up on both sides. The bottom was brushy, with scattered pines and cedars, but not by any means impassible. The smashed and broken brush made the trail of those she pursued so plain, a Sunday School girl from Chicago could follow it.

Over the sound of her horse trampling the same brush, she finally heard the lowing of cattle ahead. Her heart quickened, pounding in her ears. She took a long, deep breath. She slowed her horse to move more quietly. She lifted the rifle from its scabbard, levered a shell into the chamber, and laid it across the saddle in front of her, resting on her legs.

Rounding a small bend she spotted her heifers. They were bunched in a clearing, tearing at the plentiful grass in the canyon bottom. She stopped, looking around for the rustlers. Alarms sounded in her mind. Why would they go to all the trouble of stealing her cattle, then just leave them grazing in the bottom of a canyon?

'Better toss that rifle on the ground!'

The sudden voice close behind her nearly caused her to jump clear out of the saddle. She whipped her head around. The first thing she saw was a cold pair of impossibly pale eyes fixed on her. She knew those eyes! She hadn't paid a lot of attention to the face before, but she knew those eyes! She remembered them from the time she had bested him in a shooting contest when she was still a girl, and he had worked a short time on the X K Bar. The last time she had seen them she had tried to put a bullet between them. She had overshot, just grazing the top of his head.

Her mind raced desperately. The reality of her stupidity, riding into a trap like this washed over her, leaving her weak with sudden chagrin and despair. Because she could think of nothing else to do, she used her left hand to lift the rifle from her legs. As she lifted it, she tried to furtively slide her right hand across so she could draw her pistol. If she could get it out of the holster before the rustler saw what she was doing, she might be able to whirl and shoot before he could use that rifle.

'Don't even try that!' he snapped, his voice slapping against her like a wet glove across the face. 'You touch that gun and I'll blow your shoulder apart.'

She nudged her horse with her heel to make him turn more toward her antagonist. Even as she did, she complied and dropped the rifle onto the ground. When the stock hit the ground it fired, the bullet sailing harmlessly into the air.

'Hair trigger on that rifle,' the outlaw commented. 'Kinda dangerous haulin' around a loaded rifle with a hair trigger like that. Somebody might get hurt.'

Fighting for control of her own emotions if not the situation, she blurted, 'What are you doing with my cattle? Why have you brought them clear down here?'

Unexpectedly he laughed quietly. There was no humor in the laugh. It sent a sudden shiver running through her. 'You're a little late wonderin' about that. Fact is, bein' able to sell them is just gonna be a little extra bonus. The real reason was just to get you to follow 'em. And sure enough, here you are. All by yourself. Now just use a thumb and one finger of your left hand, and lift that pistol outa the holster and drop it beside the rifle.' Louellen hesitated until he barked, 'Now!'

She did as he demanded, feeling suddenly defenseless. Only her mother knew where she was. By the time she could send help, it would be far too late to do her any good. She had walked into a trap any girl would have known better than to fall for.

No sooner had her pistol hit the ground than he said, 'By the way, my name's Leif. Just in case you don't remember. You'll for sure remember it now anyway, seein' as how we're gonna get to know each other real good. Real good. Now head that horse to your left and follow that little trail that leads off there.'

'Where are we going?'

That same chilling laugh threatened to freeze her lungs so she couldn't breathe. 'Oh, there's a cabin that nobody but us boys uses no more just up the draw a ways. That there's gonna be our little love nest, sweet-heart, where you get to pay me back for this scar on my head, and for makin' me round up another bunch o' guys for my outfit. The boys'll take these heifers on a ways an' sell 'em, while you an' me are havin' the time of our lives. Now move!'

The last words were barked with such ferocity she cringed. She didn't respond quickly enough. He rode up beside her and lashed her with a braided quirt she hadn't even noticed he held in his left hand. It whipped across the back of her shoulders. White hot fire shot across her back. She cried out in surprise and pain.

'Shut up an' get movin', or you'll get a whole lot more o' that!' he threatened.

He raised the quirt to strike again. Steeling herself against the agony of the welt already rising against the back of her shirt, she reined her horse around and nudged him along the narrow trail. Leif fell in close behind her.

Less than half a mile later they rode into a clearing.

A surprisingly well-built little cabin sat in the center. It clearly had not been abandoned long. There was no way she could fight against the lash of that quirt, let alone Leif's strength or his gun. That quirt hurt worse than anything she had ever felt in her life. Random and out of place, she suddenly felt ashamed she had ever used one on a horse.

That did nothing to alleviate the desperation of her situation. Nobody knew where she was. The door of that snug little cabin loomed before her like the gate of hell. The hell she had walked into, and from which she knew with absolute certainty there was no escape.

CHAPTER 20

'Now get down off that horse!'

The outlaw's voice, laden with months of pent-up fury and frustration, slapped at Louellen with mind-assaulting force. The fierce, vindictive wrath in his tone threatened to knock her from the saddle by its very brutishness. She half fell, half dismounted and staggered as her feet hit the ground. He shoved her toward the cabin door, nearly knocking her down once again.

She grabbed the edge of the door for balance as she stumbled across the threshold. The inside of the cabin was dim and cool, away from the harsh glare of the sun. Instead of feeling like entering a shelter, it felt as if she were thrust into some cave of deep despair. She blinked rapidly, trying to adjust her eyes to the dim interior.

The inside of the cabin consisted of a bunk built along each of the four walls. A stove stood in the center of the floor, with a table to one side. Opposite the table a free-standing cupboard was cluttered with dirty pans and skillets. Trash was strewn about the floor. Each of the bunks was covered with a pile of dirty wool blankets.

'What … what is this place?' she stammered.

Leif's laugh sounded like a rasp grating across the ends of nails. 'Just a spot us boys like to use now an' then,' he explained.

'Use … for what?' she demanded, striving desperately to use words to stall until she could think of some way of escape. Or maybe some way to delay the inevitable.

'You don't even know where we're at, do you?' he asked, suddenly intrigued, caught up in a sudden urge to taunt her.

'No.'

He gave a harsh, single-syllable laugh. 'You been trailin' them cows o' yours this whole ways, and you don't have no least idea where you're at? What a stupid little twit you turned out to be!'

She stared at him with total incomprehension. He tilted his head back and laughed far more raucously than the occasion called for. 'Where'd you plow this groove into my forehead, you danged spitfire?'

As he said it, he whipped off his hat and pulled the hair aside from his forehead, revealing a still red, heavily scabbed wound nearly three inches long.

Her mind refused to grasp his meaning. Her head roared. Her heart pounded in her ears. She couldn't think. She could only imagine the things he was about to do to her. She knew with sudden certainty that he would kill her when he had finished with her. He had no choice. If he left her alive to be a witness against him, his life would be worth nothing in the whole country.

His patience abruptly ran out. 'This here's a spot me'n the boys use while we're waitin' for a stage to come along with a load o' cash. It's just down that draw past that brush that you'll come out right in Red Canyon,' he explained, his voice an exaggerated drawl with mocking tones, as if explaining the alphabet to a slow child. 'Red Canyon. Remember that place, Red? I been figuring ever since you knocked me off o' my horse there how to get you back here. I figured the best place to get even with you could only be the same spot. Good old Red Canyon! Now you come here!'

As he said it he grabbed the front of her shirt and jerked her toward himself, bending down toward her lips as she was propelled helplessly nearer to his own.

Some feverishly working portion of her brain flashed an image of Dolly, as she disabled the outlaw with a gun at the stagecoach. Without even thinking what she was doing, Louellen used the impetus of her momentum toward him instead of resisting. She lifted a knee into his groin with every ounce of strength she could muster.

Air exploded from his mouth as he doubled forward. His eyes jerked open as widely as his mouth. As though those too-wide orbs invited the act, she jammed fingers into both of those stunned spheres. She was rewarded by a squeal not unlike a stuck pig.

She whirled and fled through the door. She leaped into the saddle and kicked her horse into a run, steering him directly into the brush that lined the draw behind the cabin. Oblivious to the noise and the clear trail she was leaving behind, she ran the horse headlong, desperate to escape the certain fate that loomed behind her.

In the deep shadows of the trees thirty yards from the cabin, an unseen form held a rifle against a tree to steady it. The sights were trained on Mortenson's chest. The finger tightened on the trigger. As Louellen fled, the unseen watcher swore under his breath and lowered his gun.

Gasping, staggering, unable to stand straight, trying to swipe the copious flood of tears from his violated eyes, trying frantically to clear his vision, Leif lunged from the cabin and swung onto his own horse. Jamming spurs into the animal's sides, he was confident it would follow the other horse, without his guidance. Unfortunately for Louellen, he was exactly right.

Blindly, he pulled his rifle from its scabbard and levered a shell into the chamber, cursing with a quiet ferocity that left no doubt of the savagery of his boiling anger.

The agony between his legs dragged continuous groans from his throat between the half-whispered curses. From time to time his vision cleared enough to catch a glimpse of the fleeing woman. Only the obedience of a horse, worthy of a far better master, enabled him to stay on her trail.

A hundred yards ahead of him, Louellen bent low over the saddle horn, endured the lashes and scratches of innumerable branches and twigs, unaware of the sobs that were torn constantly from her throat. Suddenly the way opened before her. The brush thinned. The sides of the draw receded on both sides. She galloped out into the greater openness of Red Canyon.

Desperately she cast her eyes back and forth, searching for somebody, some place, some stage station, some ranch house, any sign of civilization or any people. Her mind screamed, Help! Help! Someone! Anyone! Save me!

Behind her Leif broke into the open as well. He jerked the rifle to his shoulder. He swiped a sleeve across his still-watering, stinging eyes. He managed an instant's vision adequate to see his sights. The rifle barked and kicked against his shoulder.

Louellen's horse broke stride and went down. She heard the gunshot even as she managed to jerk her leg from the stirrup to keep it from being caught beneath the falling steed. She hit the ground hard, driving the wind from her lungs. She lunged to her feet, but couldn't get enough breath to run. She stood, bent over, trying valiantly to suck air into her lungs.

A hand grabbed a handful of hair and jerked her backward, slamming her onto the ground. Once again she fought to breathe, unable to draw air into her lungs. The world spun about her. She was aware, through the pain and fear, of her shirt being grabbed and ripped from her, buttons flying.

The outlaw stood with one boot on her hair, pinning her head to the ground. Using both hands and both sleeves, he kept wiping his eyes until their pain and watering lessened enough to let him see.

Red squirmed, grabbed at his leg, tried everything

141

to no avail to free her hair that was pinned fast to the ground. Then Leif's weight was suddenly heavy on top of her, pressing her down, pinning her to the earth. His breath was fetid in her nostrils. His hands groped her crudely, hungrily. There was no place left to run, even if she had the ability to run. Her options had run out. She faced nothing but the full measure of his hatred, lust and vengeance. All hope of escape was gone.

Had she been able to see, that same shadowy figure once again stood in the shelter of the trees, his rifle trained on Mortenson. But if he intended to be her savior, why didn't he shoot?

CHAPTER 21

Louellen was not out of the yard before Little Earl exited the barn aboard Chipper, his pinto gelding. He rode bareback. His father had promised to make tapaderos for a saddle 'one of these days' to be sure the boy couldn't get hung up in a stirrup if he fell off, or got thrown off, a horse. For now, he rode bareback.

Though the pinto wasn't large, neither was Little Earl. Astride the animal, his legs stuck out almost straight sideways. That made him look awkward, but he rode the horse as if he were part of its hide.

He had a switch in his right hand. He used it now to whip the horse from side to side with every stride, urging him to the greatest possible speed. He bent forward over the horse's neck, repeating a litany of 'C'mon, Chipper, faster. We gotta go faster,' over and over.

Shannon Creed saw the small dust cloud first. He turned from what he was doing and rode toward it, noting almost automatically it was someone coming from the direction of the X K Bar. Nearly half a mile away he recognized it as Little Earl.

His stomach tied into a knot. Nothing but trouble would bring the boy riding 'hell-for-leather' as he certainly was. As they drew closer to each other he noted the horse was sweating heavily, with bits of foam whipping from the ends of the bridle bit to fly away in the breeze.

As they drew close, Little Earl began to saw at the reins, yelling, 'Whoa now, Chipper!' even as the animal came to a stop in a series of stiff-legged, jolting lunges.

'What's wrong?' Creed demanded.

'It's Red! She's done got her bedroll an' lit out after some rustlers all by herself!' Little Earl shouted, much too loud for his nearness.

'She what?!'

The boy repeated the statement, word for word.

'When?'

'Just as long ago as it took me to ride over here to your place.'

'How does she know there's rustlers?'

'She run onto their tracks. Then she hightailed it home to get her bedroll, and told her ma she was goin' after 'em.'

'And her mother let her go?'

'Nossir. Not exactly. Well, I guess she sorta did. She just couldn't stop her. She tried to get her to ride over to where the crew's workin' them cows over west, but she wasn't listenin' to nothin'. She said by the time she did that, they'd have the heifers they stole plumb outa the country or sold an' butchered. She said it was up to her and she wasn't gonna let no … uh, well, I can't rightly say what she called 'em … but she said she wasn't gonna let 'em steal her blind.'

Shannon's mind raced. He forced himself to a calm he certainly didn't feel. 'Do you know where the tracks are?'

'Yessir. Well, pretty close. I snucked up and listened when Red was arguin' with her ma. You know that draw a couple miles southwest o' the house? The one with the funny shaped rocks stickin' up right in the middle?'

'I know the place.'

'You goin' after her?'

'You better believe it. How long will it take you to get to the rest of the crew and send them after me?'

'Not near as long as you think. Flint, he left Anton to stay on the place. I told him what was happenin' and asked him to go get the crew. He'll likely have 'em headin' straight for there, but they're quite a ways over west. It'll take 'em a while.'

'Well, give your horse a little breather, then head back and see if you can catch up with them. Don't go runnin' your horse to death, though. Pay attention to 'im, and push 'im as much as you can without overdoin' it. Can you do that?'

'Sure thing, Mr. Creed.'

'OK. Tell them what's happening, and tell them I'm riding hard to catch up to her. Maybe I can catch up with her before she catches up with them.'

Without waiting for an answer Shannon jabbed his spurs in his horse's sides. He lifted him to a smooth, ground-eating lope, heading for the spot the boy had identified.

He found the tracks with no trouble from the boy's direction. Those tracks told a story as clearly as if written on paper. It was instantly obvious that they were left in such a way as to make it impossible for Louellen not to see and follow them. If 'TRAP' had been scratched into the dirt their purpose could not have been more obvious. Shivers ran up and down his back. His stomach cramped. He swallowed with difficulty. He wasn't sure whether to swear or sob. Whatever he did, he knew it would be too little, too late.

'Mortenson!' he said aloud. 'It's that worthless, cold-blooded Leif Mortenson, just as sure as anything. I should have recognized those eyes of his at the stage-coach. I for sure saw him watchin' Red in town. I've been almost sure it was him that I saw tracks of, watchin' her and the crew workin' cows. Sure as anything it was. He was just watchin' and waitin', bidin' his time till he could leave a trail she'd follow without the rest of the crew. He's picked up a couple of bad apples to replace some o' the ones we killed, and he's out for revenge on Red. And I've let it happen. I've let it happen. It's all my fault. I've let it happen.'

The tracks told the story of a good sized bunch of bred heifers being herded by four riders. That much he had already found. What sent even deeper chills of fear through him was that other set of tracks. He had followed them from the ranch many times. He had picked them up at various places and followed them, keeping an eye on Louellen. He was a tracker. He knew those tracks by heart.

'That stupid, lame-brained girl!' he expostulated. 'After what she's been through, she's gotta know better'n to pull a danged-fool stunt like this!'

Without slowing the horse's gait he followed the well-beaten trail. An hour later he slowed the horse to a swift trot, knowing the horse could keep that pace almost indefinitely, so long as he stopped to give him water and a bait of oats at regular intervals. Even if he had to ride the horse to death, it was imperative that he pursue his quarry as fast as humanly possible.

'I'm gonna take that worthless piece of horse dung apart bit by bit when I get a hold of him!' he promised himself. Even as he said it, he knew whatever he did to Leif would be of no help or relief to Louellen.

Near the head of French Creek he spotted where she had camped for the night. He didn't slow down.

Three miles farther he saw where the rustlers had camped for the night as well. He knew he couldn't be more than an hour or two behind them. Even so, he knew he was far, far too late. Whatever the outlaws had in mind, they had more than enough time before he could interfere.

He didn't even hear the sob of despair that was torn from his lips with every stride of his horse.

CHAPTER 22

Taking in the tell-tale signs at a glance, Shannon scarcely slowed at the cabin. His heart surged, threatening to burst through the barrier of ribs and flesh.

'She's got away from him somehow!' he exulted. 'Go, Red! Go! Stay ahead of him just a little bit longer. I'm coming, sweetheart! I'm coming!'

He followed the trail of smashed and broken brush through the narrow draw, looking neither left nor right, caution long since left in the other detritus of the trail.

He broke into the open unexpectedly. He grunted in surprise, instinctively recognizing Red Kenyon. His eyes instantly froze on the struggling pair on the ground.

She's still fightin' 'im, his mind roared in fierce pride and joy. Instantly, a second voice, more reasoned, shouted in his mind, Can't shoot. I'll hit Red.

Some part of his attention noted half her clothes were torn off. The pair grappling on the ground were totally unaware of his approach. At a dead run his spent, exhausted horse passed by the two. As he did, Creed left the saddle in a long dive. His shoulder connected with the outlaw just as he raised up and started a backhand swing aimed at Red's face. He was lifted clear of the ground by the force of the impact when Creed's body smashed into him.

As the outlaw hit the ground, Creed rolled clear and struggled to his feet. To his surprise, Leif was also regaining his feet. His face was a mask of rage and hatred. He lunged at Shannon, intent on driving him to the ground.

Instead of dodging or backing away, Shannon stepped forward to meet the other's charge. He loosed a straight right fist that connected with the outlaw's chin with the sound of a sledge hammer crashing into a side of hanging beef.

Mortenson's eyes crossed. His knees buckled. He fell forward, his face smashing a small clump of sage brush.

Ignoring his down, presumably unconscious opponent, Creed rushed to Louellen. 'It's all right, Red! It's all right. I'm here!'

She stared uncomprehendingly at him a long heartbeat. She blinked rapidly several times. She emitted a long ululating wail that ended in a choked sob. She reached out both arms to him, unaware or uncaring of her state of undress. He dropped to his knees and wrapped his arms around her.

She hugged him fiercely, frantically, as if to reassure herself that his presence was real.

'I'm here, sweetheart,' he kept repeating, as if incapable of putting any more thoughts into words.

After a long time that was less than an instant, she eased the grip with which she clung to him. 'Oh, Shannon, I'm so sorry. I'm so glad. I was such a fool. I just knew there was no way you could come. I … oh darling, I…'

With a squeal she lunged sideways, jerking Shannon with her. He fell headlong on his side in the grass.

Even as he was falling, some part of his mind heard the angry whine of a bullet whipping past his ear. An instant later the report of a .45 slammed against that ear.

Somehow Leif had regained consciousness. His vision still blurred by the force of the blow that felled him, he fired again, wildly shooting high and wide.

Acting on pure instinct, Creed rolled to one side, whipped out his gun and fired three times in rapid succession. All three bullets found their mark with the characteristic splat of lead smashing its way through flesh.

Leif stared at him, unmoving. His lips were curled back from his teeth, looking more like an animal snarl than any human expression. The expression didn't change. The eerily pale eyes never changed their focus. Something behind the eyes simply faded away, leaving them as empty as the soul of the man he had always been. He fell forward onto his face.

Creed took a deep breath and let it out slowly. 'Dang, he was tough,' he muttered.

The shadow in the timber swore and once again lowered his rifle.

By habit he thumbed out the spent cartridges from his .45, replacing them with fresh ones. He looked at Louellen, realizing for the first time the immodesty of her condition. He started to say something when dirt kicked up two feet to his left. At almost the same moment the whang of a rifle shot reached them as well.

Shannon lunged forward, knocking Louellen to the ground. 'Stay down!' he commanded. 'There's a couple more out there somewhere.'

Her only response was another small sob, but she flattened herself against the ground.

Looking around, Shannon spotted a small hollow that offered a modicum of cover. 'Crawl over there and make yourself as small as possible,' he ordered.

She scrambled to comply. Another bullet whined in the air above them.

Swiftly, Shannon crabbed his way back to the dead outlaw and grabbed his pistol. He crawled back, handing it to Louellen. 'Stay flat and listen close. If you hear anyone sneakin' up on you, play dead till you know where they are. Then shoot. Don't say nothin'. Just shoot. OK?'

She nodded mutely. She started to say something, but he was gone. She strained to hear him, but no sound came to her. She shivered, whether with cold or fear mattered nothing. She forced herself to be still and listen.

Shannon belly-crawled to a shallow ditch that led back the way they had come. With its depression to cover his movements, he crawled as rapidly as possible without making any noise. When he had covered nearly two hundred yards, he stopped to listen.

For quite a while he heard nothing. Then a whispered voice said, 'Where'd they go?'

'They gotta be right there,' the whispered answer responded. 'There ain't nowhere they could go without us seein' 'em.'

'Just keep your eyes peeled. They'll move sooner or later.'

Fixing their position by their whispered conversation, Creed silently crawled past them. A dozen yards beyond them, he stood up.

Spread flat in the grass and brush, two men watched the last spot they had seen him over the barrels of their rifles. Shannon almost grinned.

'You boys lookin' for me?' he asked in a cheerful, conversational tone.

The effect was electric. For the barest instant the pair froze in place. Then they leaped to their feet, whipping their rifles around. Their eyes were too wide open. Their mouths were clenched. Their lips were thin lines in bloodless faces. Their effort to turn and shoot was far, far too slow.

Midway in his swing toward their adversary, one's body jerked and flopped backward. In almost the same instant the other issued a gurgling gasp. As he did, he appeared to throw his rifle skyward. It discharged as it left his hand. Both of the rustlers were dead when the ground reached up to wrap them in a final embrace.

Creed lifted his voice. 'I got 'em both, Red. You can

put down the gun. For cryin' out loud, don't go shootin' me.'

In answer Red laughed, a small titter that almost trembled from her lips. Then it seemed to grow of its own volition. It turned into a chuckle, then a full laugh. Then it rose in intensity until she was howling hysterically.

As soon as she answered, Shannon began to walk swiftly toward her. By the time her laugh had swollen into its hysterical and meaningless wail, he was beside her. He lifted her up and enfolded her in his embrace. He buried his face in her hair, whispering into her ear.

'It's all right now, sweetheart. You're safe now.'

Slowly her sobbing laughter subsided. She took a deep, ragged breath. He released her and stepped back.

'I got an extra shirt in my bedroll,' he said. 'I'll get it for you.'

She looked down at herself, realizing for the first time how exposed she was. She hurriedly crossed her arms over her breasts, her face suddenly as red as her hair.

Deliberately turning his back, Creed walked to his horse and retrieved his extra shirt from his bedroll. He walked backward as he took it to her, handing it out behind himself. When he was within reach she grabbed it and hurriedly put it on.

'OK,' she announced. 'You can turn around now.'

He did. He looked her up and down, hungrily taking in every detail. Dirty, disheveled, bruised, blood oozing from half a dozen scratches, she was the most beautiful thing he had ever seen in his life.

'Would you mind if I kiss the woman who's going to be my wife?' he asked abruptly.

'If that's me, you better hurry up about it,' she retorted.

He did.

CHAPTER 23

The end is not always the end. Believing something has come to an end when it has not can be hazardous, even fatal. One of history's great ironies is the number of heroes who are felled just when they thought victory was theirs, and lowered their guard.

Sometimes even the most seasoned warriors can suffer from mind-freeze. Sometimes it is that strange phenomenon that turns victory into tragic defeat. Sometimes it has cost greater men than Shannon Creed their lives.

Shannon's senses had been heightened to a razor edge as he followed Louellen's trail. They had given him an almost super-human ability to think and act at a speed none but those specially talented man-hunters ever achieve.

He had, against all his expectations, arrived in time to rescue the woman he loved more than life itself. He had killed her assailant, and ended forever the threat of the man's hatred. He had stalked and slain the pair who thought to dispatch him from hiding.

Now he was holding the woman he loved in his arms. She had indicated a joyous willingness to be his wife. It was a fairy-tale ending to what had appeared to be a horrible tragedy in progress. Life was good.

It did not occur to him, in his euphoria, that there were four men he had been tracking. Even Louellen knew there were four of them. She had ascertained that immediately when she had come upon the tracks.

Creed knew that as well. Four men. That meant Mortenson and three others he had recruited.

He had killed Mortenson.

He had killed the two who laid out in the grass to shoot both him and Louellen from ambush.

He simply forgot to count all the way to four.

One. Two. Three. We must be done now.

There was a fourth man that had given Dolly the creeps nearly as badly as Mortenson himself. He was a small man. He was young, almost boyish. His teeth were crooked, so when he smiled it was almost a snaggle-toothed sneer. He was also cunning, sneaky and almost inhumanly mean.

One of the soiled doves at the Sundown Saloon had been warned against being available to the youngster. She had done so anyway, and been unable to work for nearly a week. The man took perverse delight in inflicting pain and injury. He had held a hand over her mouth so none would hear her scream as he exacted excruciating pain on her, all while smiling that crooked-toothed grin.

Unbeknownst to any of the others, he had already decided to kill the other three when they had abducted Louellen and secured her at the cabin. Accordingly he had separated himself from the others. He was on the verge of shooting Leif from the cover of the trees by the cabin when Louellen had made her unexpected escape.

When Leif managed to hobble to his horse and pursue his prey, the young man hung back, watching and waiting. Once again he was in position, taking aim to dispatch Mortenson, when Shannon burst on the scene like an avenging demon, and took care of Leif for him.

'Well, that's one bullet I can save,' the young man grinned viciously.

He was again positioned, his finger on the trigger, to take out Creed from the same cover. To his surprise, someone fired at his intended target a split-second before he would have done so. One of those he had teamed with to steal the heifers was lying in the grass, shooting poorly.

'How could you miss from that range, Studemeyer?' he sneered.

Even as he breathed the words, a second rifle right beside Studemeyer barked. That would be Smith. Or so he said. One more Smith unrelated to all the other Smiths that roamed the country. No matter. He couldn't care less what anyone's real name was. He just wanted that spitfire of a woman.

He watched, bemused, as Creed skillfully circumnavigated the hiding spot of the pair, stepped up behind them, and shot them both.

Creed didn't shoot them as he, himself would have. There was no reason in the world to say anything, to give them warning, to allow them a chance to surrender. That was just stupid. He was behind them. They didn't know he was there. He could kill them in half a second before they even knew he was there.

For whatever reason, the guy named Creed refused to do so. The end result was the same, so what did it matter?

Just as a matter of amusement he watched as Shannon called out to Louellen, then ran to where she lay hidden in the grass. He enjoyed the view as they embraced. He watched, bemused, as Creed hurried to his bedroll and got a shirt for the woman to put on. How touching! Oh well. That would just give him one more thing to enjoy removing after she watched the interfering idiot die.

He raised his rifle, placing the sights dead center in the man's chest. His finger tightened on the trigger. He smiled wickedly, already ravishing that redhead in his mind.

Something smashed into his back, slamming him into the tree against which he rested his rifle. His mind whirled, trying to discern what happened. He tried to take a breath, but felt as if that ability had been driven from him. Something had hit him from behind. He tried to turn to figure out what it was. Whatever it was slammed into him again. Then again almost instantly.

He couldn't force himself to turn. He tried, but

his body wouldn't obey his orders. The tree he had been slammed against wasn't in front of him anymore. Nothing was in front of him. Nothing but a strange wall of blackness that seemed to be enfolding him.

He felt nothing. He was just confused. Then it didn't matter.

A hundred yards away, on the heels of an unexpected gunshot, Shannon grabbed Louellen and shoved her to the ground, covering her with his own body. Two more rifle shots followed in rapid succession. He frowned, trying to divine the source.

Then he saw somebody flop backward from a tree at the edge of the timber and fall to the ground. He did not move.

'You all right, Creed?' a voice called.

'That you, Flint?'

'Yeah. Me'n the boys.'

'Was that you shootin'?'

'Yeah. Some fella was pullin' down on you from that tree yonder.'

Shannon's mind raced. Who could that have been? He had killed Mortenson. He had killed both of Mortenson's men that were trying to kill him from ambush.

Both? Two of them and one of Mortenson. That's three. There were four sets of tracks! There was a fourth rustler!

He mentally slapped himself alongside his head. How could he have possibly been so stupid as to lose count of his foes? He knew a long string of men who had died for lesser mistakes.

Trying to hide his confusion and discomfiture, he called out, 'How'd you boys get here so quick?'

'Little Earl rode his horse pert near to death gettin' to us. Then we rode ours pert near to death as well. Seems like we got here just in the nick of time.'

'You couldn't have cut it much closer,' Shannon agreed.

In the days and years to come he would give fervent thanks for that split-second timing a hundred times over. Without that whole series of near miracles, they'd never have managed to merge the two ranches together. Or bring those four rambunctious redheads as unmanageable as their hair into the world.